RUN
FOR
YOUR
LIFE

RUN FOR YOUR LIFE

TREVOR KEW

James Lorimer & Company Ltd., Publishers
Toronto

James Lorimer & Company Ltd., Publishers acknowledges the support of the Ontario Arts Council (OAC), an agency of the Government of Ontario, which in 2015-16 funded 1,676 individual artists and 1,125 organizations in 209 communities across Ontario for a total of $50.5 million. We acknowledge the support of the Canada Council for the Arts, which last year invested $153 million to bring the arts to Canadians throughout the country. This project has been made possible in part by the Government of Canada and with the support of the Ontario Media Development Corporation.

Cover design: Tyler Cleroux
Cover image: iStock

Library and Archives Canada Cataloguing in Publication

Kew, Trevor, author
    Run for your life / Trevor Kew.

(Sports stories)
Issued in print and electronic formats.
ISBN 978-1-4594-1190-6 (paperback).--ISBN 978-1-4594-1192-0 (epub)

    I. Title. II. Series: Sports stories (Toronto, Ont.)

PS8621.E95R85 2017   jC813'.6   C2016-906034-9
                                              C2016-906035-7

Published by: Distributed by:
James Lorimer & Company Ltd.,   Formac Lorimer Books
Publishers   5502 Atlantic Street
117 Peter Street, Suite 304   Halifax, NS, Canada
Toronto, ON, Canada   B3H 1G4
M5V 0M3
www.lorimer.ca

Printed and bound in Canada.
Manufactured by Friesens Corporation in Altona, Manitoba, Canada in January 2017.
Job #229615

*For Tony, who began walking, and running,
as this book found its feet.*

Contents

PROLOGUE

The path is never straight, never flat — never easy. The soft black dirt crumbles under the soles of my shoes. Thick roots stretch out like sneaky legs, trying to catch my toes. Wet green leaves reach out to slap me in the face.

One big soggy fern gets me really good as I skid around a corner. *Whap* — right in the kisser. Eyes stinging, I wipe my face on my T-shirt. But I don't stop running, not for a second.

Faster, faster — you've got to go faster.

If I slow down, *they* will catch me.

The cedar trees here are like skyscrapers. They rise up until they vanish into the mist. A really big one blocks the path in front of me. There is no way around it, but I know the secrets of this trail. With the light of the evening sun fading fast, I run straight ahead, picking up speed.

A gap appears at the base of the big tree, under its massive roots. The gap is round, like the entrance to an animal's cave. As I squeeze my body through, I can smell the damp bark of the tree. And then I pop out the other side like a rabbit.

Both feet land on a steep slope leading down, down —

Splash! I am in the creek before I see it. But it is not deep enough this time of year to turn me from a runner into a swimmer. When I splash onto the opposite bank, my running shoes have transformed into a pair of soggy clogs.

I can't let that stop me. Feet scrabbling, hands grasping, I drag myself up to the crest of a long hill.

It is me against the forest. I don't mean slappy ferns and slippery roots and chilly creeks. Here, now, alone, I am running for my life. Beneath the thumping of my heart, I hear the pounding of feet. *They* are after me. With the shadows growing longer around me, I sense how close they are.

Faster, faster — you've got to go faster.

My shoes skid over a long, flat, greasy-wet stone. Arms waving like a toddler on skates, I catch myself right at the edge of the path. I look down. A steep rocky gorge slopes down to the creek. Falling would not have been pretty.

But maybe the fear is just what I need to get my heavy feet moving again. Clenching my teeth, I duck under a row of low branches and surge forward.

The skin on the back of my neck tingles. Is it just

the chill of the forest air? No — it is the icy breath of my pursuers. They are right behind me now, closing in.

Up ahead, through the dripping dark green of the forest, a light appears.

For a traveller, the first sight of home is a relief. For a runner, nothing is more dangerous. This is where *they* catch you. You relax just when you should be going for broke, straining every muscle to the end.

As the path becomes a dirt road, I break into a full sprint. My eyes are focused forward, my mind on what is right behind me.

Faster, faster — you've got to go faster.

Go, go.

Run for your life.

1 ROCKET FUEL

At home, the beam of the backyard light greets me. I can see the short, chubby, familiar shape of a man standing behind the barbecue.

"Hey, look who's back. We were just going to send out a search party."

Dad is rotating skewers of meat on the grill with the concentration of a nuclear scientist. But the goofy grin on his face makes him look more like the Cheshire cat from *Alice in Wonderland*.

Mom is sitting in a folding chair on the other side of the yard. The ice-blue light of the phone in her hand reflects off her face. Looking up in my direction, she puts the phone in her pocket.

"Good run, Chris?"

I gulp down some air, my chest heaving. "Pretty good. The creek slowed me down a bit. But I managed to get going again."

She shakes her head. "I can't even manage to go jogging more than once a week. And it's barely a jog — more of a bouncy stroll. I don't know how you do it. When you get tired — how do you keep going?"

I shrug. I've never told anyone what I think about when I run, not even my parents. They might worry about me. Parents are so worried these days from the stories they hear on the news. Sure, there are kids out there who mix up fantasy and reality. But I'm just a boring thirteen-year-old guy. I don't think video games are more important than life. I don't believe in ghosts or demons or magic spells. And I know that when I run, those shadowy things aren't really there. But I still need them. They keep me going. I know the only way to run faster is to run for your life.

Fat sizzles on the barbecue. Dad turns the skewers once more. "I don't know why you couldn't take a couple of days off, my son. Go fishing. Go to the movies. Relax."

"Yeah, Chris," says a squeaky little voice. "Relax."

A flood of giggles erupts from inside the house. A small girl with long dark hair sticks her head out through the doorway.

"Hi, Sarah," I say.

"Re-*lax*," she repeats, sticking her tongue out at me.

An identical face appears beside her.

"Lucy!" I shout.

"Chris!" she cries, waving wildly.

My sisters jostle their way through the doorway,

grunting like bear cubs. Sarah heads straight for Dad, standing so close to the grill that he has to reach out and hold her back. Lucy trots over and punches me in the thigh.

"Ow!" I yelp. "Jeez — someone's getting stronger."

Lucy parks herself on the edge of Mom's lawn chair. In an instant, she has Mom's phone in her hands and is tapping away at the screen.

"Not now, Lucy," Mom says, taking the phone and putting it back in her pocket. "You know the rule. No phones at mealtimes."

Dad is always telling Mom to forget about work for five minutes and put her phone away. But right now, he just lifts the skewers from the grill and places them on a big platter. He carries them to the wooden picnic table in the centre of the yard and motions for us to come sit down.

"Yum, yum," says Sarah.

"Pig's bum," says Lucy.

"Actually," says Dad, "it's lamb and chicken."

Along with the skewers come a heap of vegetables and a big bowl of yogurt. In the middle of the table, as always, there is a plate of warm flatbread.

"Dig in," he says.

Sometimes it annoys me that my dad has no passions apart from his belly. But this is not one of those times. Ripping off a piece of flatbread, I use it to pull two chunks of chicken from a skewer and ram the food into my mouth. I close my eyes. I'm pretty sure that nothing has ever tasted this good.

A few minutes later, Dad stands up and walks back over to the grill.

"Who wants seconds?"

My hand shoots up in the air. "Me!"

Dad takes my empty plate and returns it full.

Mom points to the food. "Fuel for the big race next week, eh, Chris?"

"Mhmm," I mumble through a mouthful of meat and bread.

She holds up a skewer of lamb from her plate. "Jet fuel."

I hold up one of mine. "Rocket fuel."

As he sits down, Dad shakes his head. "I don't understand you two sometimes. How can you describe something as wonderful as food as nothing but fuel? Especially my beautiful kebabs."

Sarah and Lucy have slipped away from the table. They are bouncing a big red ball back and forth. I snatch up a half-eaten chicken skewer off Sarah's plate.

"Relax," I tell my dad. "It's not every cook that can make rocket fuel taste this good."

2 DISTANT FIRES

At Oak Bay Secondary School, a long outdoor staircase leads from the main building to the gym. From the top of those stairs, I can see the small forest behind the playing fields. Everyone calls it the Jungle. There are running trails that cut back and forth through the Jungle. That is where our cross-country team trains three times a week.

"Hey — wait up!"

I hear the slap of shoes on the concrete stairs behind me. Something slams against my elbow.

"Hey." I turn and see a small freckly kid wearing a massive backpack. "Watch it."

"What's up, Big K?" he says.

Big K? Where did he get that from? I guess I am tall, at least compared to him. And my last name is Khalili, though it doesn't start with a *K* sound. The *Kh* is a sort of growling sound that you make in the back of your throat. Not one person at school has a clue how to pronounce it.

"Give it up, Sparky," I tell him.

Greg Sparks has been trying to lose his nickname for years. It hasn't worked. Even the teachers call him Sparky. It's not that he is a bad guy or anything. He's all right. He's just a bit too *sparky* sometimes, on *and* off the race track.

Together, we walk down the steps to the gym. The boys' locker room is so full that it is hard to find a place to sit down. Half the soccer team is in there, and the whole basketball team, including my buddy Yongwon.

"Hey, what's up, Chris?" says Yongwon, tugging a practice jersey on over his head.

"We're calling him Big K now," says Sparky.

Yongwon shakes his head. "No, we're not, Sparky."

I sit down and start to get changed.

"Coach says we're running wind-sprints today," says a guy next to Yongwon. "Double for anyone who's late."

Yongwon groans. "Man, that guy loves to make us run. We hardly touched the basketballs at all last week. I might as well quit the team and join cross-country."

"You wouldn't last five minutes," I tell him, bending down to tie my laces.

"Not even *one* minute," says Sparky.

"Chill out, Sparky."

Yongwon shrugs. "Guess I'd better get to practice. No double wind-sprints for me, thanks. Later, guys."

"Later," I say.

"Peace out," says Sparky, which makes me cringe a little.

Once we have both changed into our running stuff, Sparky and I leave together. Out on the playing fields, the boys and girls soccer teams are warming up. We make sure to jog around the side where the girls are. Girls don't go crazy for the guys on the cross-country team like they do for soccer or basketball players. But I think I see one or two girls glancing in my direction. Or is that just wishful thinking?

Forget it. I need to focus. The qualifying race for the Victoria city finals is this Saturday. I have to be ready. This is no time to slack off.

On the far side of the fields, a group of girls and boys in running shorts have gathered. A tall blonde woman with a clipboard stands in front of them with her back to the Jungle.

"Greg Sparks, Christopher Khalili — you're late," she says. In her Australian accent, my name sounds like Christopher Carlyle, or Christopher Kiley, or something like that.

"Sorry, Coach Clark," I say, thinking fast. "We had a math test —"

"— French quiz," Sparky blurts out.

"Uh huh," she says. She jots something down on the clipboard.

Sparky is already huffing and puffing from the jog around the field. It's not that he's slow, but he tends to get tired out. This is hardly surprising, given the way that he runs. It's sort of halfway between a runaway train and a baby giraffe. Someone should tell him to bend his knees.

"What I was saying," begins Coach Clark, "is that today we are going to run in pairs, to work on pacing."

Something in my throat lurches and I cough awkwardly. Coach Clark glares in my direction.

It is nice, I guess, to have a real cross-country coach. Up until now, our coaches have just been teachers who couldn't coach anything else. Coach Clark is different. She ran a marathon last year, I heard, and did a triathlon the year before. I am just not into all this team stuff she wants to do. I don't run for anyone else. I run to win. If I wanted to be on a team, I would play basketball with Yongwon.

"Remember," continues Coach Clark, "the point today is not to run as fast as you can. The point is to stick together. Right — let's get going. Phones out. You've all downloaded the new pacing app, right?"

Oh, and that is another thing. She is into all this running technology. I don't use it. I am old school. I don't run to beat the clock. I run to be first to the finish line.

All around us, kids are pairing off.

"Looks like you two slowpokes are running buddies today," says Coach Clark.

I turn toward Sparky. "All right. Come on, Sparks. But you'd better keep up with me."

There are about twenty students on the cross-country team. We are near the back of the pack when we start. Side by side, Sparky and I run toward the Jungle. For the first time, I notice how strange the sky is today. There is hardly a cloud up above, but a strange white haze hangs low on the horizon.

"That's weird," I say to Sparky. "Is that fog or something?"

He is already breathing hard, but he tries not to show it. "You haven't heard about the fires?"

"Fires?"

"The — forest — fires," he huffs. "They're up on the — north of the Island. It's been — all over the news. Don't — you know — how to use the Internet?"

Forest fires? Really? Surely the smoke wouldn't travel all the way here to Victoria. It sounds too much like a movie to be true. And it wouldn't be the first time Sparky has got something wrong off the Internet.

The two of us are dead last when we hit the entrance to the trail that cuts through the Jungle. Three girls from lower grades are a few paces ahead of us. Something inside me snaps. This is ridiculous. I need to be running. Really running. On Saturday, I have to qualify for city finals. And here I am babysitting Sparky and thinking about forest fires.

"Come on," I say. I kick down against the dirt. "Let's go."

I push, cut, and zip past the rest of the runners. To his credit, Sparky keeps up. But by the time we reach the front of the pack, his face is flushed. I can see his chest expanding and contracting like an accordion.

"See ya, Sparky," I say.

I make for a gap between two trees. My feet pound hard against the trail. Following me, Sparky and the rest of the runners fade into nothing. Soon I am far ahead. The only things behind me are the long, dark shadows of the trees.

3 A THIN PIECE OF YELLOW TAPE

The barrier is just a thin piece of yellow tape.

On my side of the tape is the world of the qualifying race. I don't notice faces, just uniforms: black, blue, and red — and our own Oak Bay green-and-gold. No one is standing still. There are too many jangling nerves. My own running shoes are dancing up and down. Bending at the waist, I reach for my toes. I pull my face toward my knees. From here, through my legs, I can see the starting line. Somehow it seems to be inching closer and closer.

On the other side of the tape is the real world. Small groups of people, mostly families of the runners, sit on chairs and benches. I see a few familiar faces, but most of them are here for students from other schools. Mom is sitting on a long wooden bench, checking her phone. One of her arms is around Sarah, whose nose is buried in a big fat book. It is loud here. Music is playing. People are cheering and calling out runners' names. But Sarah might as well be in the middle of a library. And then I see Lucy on the bench next to Mom and Sarah. Lucy stares at me with a crazy intensity. She wants me to win. I can't let her down.

It's just a thin piece of yellow tape. But the world on the other side feels far away. On this side, everything is focused on the race. The top eight runners move on to the city finals in October. But I don't want to finish eighth, or third, or second. I am not thinking about the next race. I want to win right here, right now.

"Runners — to your marks!" booms a deep male voice.

All around me, uniforms move toward the starting line. A sharp elbow bumps my left arm.

"Watch it, kid," sneers a runner in a black shirt and shorts. He is muscular for someone so thin. Still, I bet I could take him in a fight.

Focus, Chris, I tell myself. *Forget about it. Save it for the race.*

I kneel down to re-tie my shoes. I make sure the laces are as tight as possible, but not so tight that they hurt my feet. Sparky kneels down next to me and does exactly the same thing.

I look up. Coach Clark is standing on the other side of the yellow tape. She is wearing a green-and-gold track suit with white running shoes. She looks fast. I'm glad I don't have to race her today. I bet every guy in this race would be eating her dust by the end of the first lap.

"Don't go out too fast today, guys," she calls out. "Pace yourselves."

Next to Sparky is a guy with a frizzy mop of red hair. His shoes are red, too, and look like they should be attached to a rocket ship. Everything about him looks fiery and quick.

We all go quiet when we hear the announcer. "Runners — get set."

There is the sound of shoes digging into the dirt, then silence that seems to last forever.

Crack — the starter's pistol fires. We jump up like spooked deer. We stumble downhill, a pack of moving bodies. Guys bump and jostle one another for position. Every race starts like this. It's like a traffic jam at rush hour, until someone breaks free.

This happens just before we reach the place where the path veers into the trees. Four of us — me, the Man in Black, Rocket-Shoes, and Sparky — move ahead of the rest of the runners. Glancing over, I expect to see Sparky puffing like a steam train. But he isn't — not yet.

We hit a long straight stretch followed by three sharp bends in the trail. After that, the path narrows. There's no place to pass. I am in second, with Rocket-Shoes right in front of me. I can tell that Sparky and the Man in Black are still with us. I can hear the thud of their shoes on the path.

We carry on single-file, matching each other stride for stride. Our eyes peer forward at the ground in front of us, watching for loose stones and tree roots. All I want to do is get out front. Forget this pacing nonsense.

A Thin Piece of Yellow Tape

I race best when I am being chased by everyone else.

We are almost at the end of our first lap when the path widens just a little. This is the chance I have been looking for. I cut wide around Rocket-Shoes and lean hard into the corner. My right shoe skids. I nearly go down. Somehow, I stumble onward and regain my pace. Behind me there is a familiar yelp followed by the sound of someone crashing onto sticks and stones. I know who it is. I know I should probably help him. He's my teammate. But I don't look back. I keep going.

We reach the bottom of a big hill. I can hear clapping and cheering coming from the top. Someone, maybe Lucy, shouts my name. After that, the sound just blurs. Powering up the slope, arms pumping, I see the starting line in front of me. In two more laps, it will be the finish line.

Surging downhill, I charge for the trees again. It seems darker in the forest this time. It doesn't feel like the middle of the afternoon on a sunny fall day. I stare at the ground. My eyes are stinging. I wipe them on my shirtsleeve. No better. It is hard to focus on the difference between the packed earth of the path and the soft mushy ground on the sides. Up ahead are two runners, still on their first lap. Unbelievable. How slow can you go? But then I notice that they are coughing really hard. One has stopped running. He is wiping his eyes too.

"Clear the track!" I holler.

I blast right between them, bouncing off somebody's shoulder.

"Hey!"

It is hard to tell how far out in front I am. I can't see the Man in Black or Rocket-Shoes when I glance back. This is good, but it could be dangerous. There is still half of the race left to go. With no one to push me, I might slack off. But the shadows of the trees are there. And *they* are there, those dark shadowy figures. They are always behind me, pushing me.

Don't stop.

Faster, faster — you've got to go faster.

My throat is dry and my eyes are watering. But never mind. By the time I reach the top of the hill and cross the starting line again, I am absolutely flying.

"Chris!" I hear my name. "Chris!"

It spurs me on. Instead of just Mom, Coach Clark and Lucy, I imagine a whole crowd of people chanting my name. *Chris, Chris, Chris —*

"Chris — stop!"

I glance back over my shoulder. Coach Clark jumps over the yellow tape barrier. She runs toward me, waving her arms. I shake my head at her. Is she crazy? I am running the race of my life. Why on earth would I stop now?

"They're calling it off," she shouts after me. "The race has been postponed!"

4 THOSE LESS FORTUNATE

I slouch in the front seat of the car. Lucy and Sarah are nattering away behind me. Pulling my hoodie down over my ears, I turn toward the window. It makes no difference. The two high, whiny voices don't stop until we are pulling into the driveway.

After the girls hop out, Mom turns to me. "Hey, you okay?"

"Oh, I'm just great," I say, spitting out the words. "I'm wonderful. I'm so happy they cancelled the race because of some stupid little forest fire a million miles away."

Mom says nothing. She just reaches over and gives me a pat on the arm. That's the difference between Mom and Dad. Mom knows how much running matters to me. And she knows when to leave me alone.

I follow her up the driveway and into the house. My legs feel kind of wobbly. It's like that feeling you get when you step off a boat and back onto dry land. I always get it after a big race, but today, somehow the feeling is stronger. Maybe anger makes it worse.

Dad is in the living room, watching TV. Normally at this time of day, he would be in the kitchen preparing dinner. And usually when he sits on the couch, he leans back into the cushions and rests his hands on his big belly. Right now, he is on the edge of his seat, staring at the screen.

"Chris," he says, motioning toward the couch. "Come here. You've got to see this."

On the screen, a helicopter is spraying water over a clump of fiery trees. *Island Fires Continue to Spread* reads the news banner.

I sigh. Fires, fires, fires. They should do a news story on my race getting cancelled. It would probably be more interesting. But Dad is paying serious attention, so I decide to keep my mouth shut.

Then the camera cuts to a new shot. Mom gasps. Dad puts his hands in front of his face, almost like he's praying. Through the deep orange flames and thick black smoke, I can just barely make out a door, a window, and the outline of a roof.

That is no forest. It is somebody's house.

★★★

At school on Monday morning, it is strangely quiet. Students stand in tight clusters, speaking in low voices. Phones are permanently attached to palms of hands.

Their eyes fixed on screens, they click and scroll with their thumbs, hoping to find something the others do not know.

I find Yongwon and the other basketball guys hanging around near the entrance to the gym. Yongwon nods at me as I walk over. The other guys barely look up.

"I hear people died."

Derek Anderson is one of those thirteen-year-olds who already looks like a grown man. He is not the tallest kid in our grade, but he is the only one with real muscles. Man muscles. On the court, he is the starting point guard and runs the team. Off the court, he runs the team too.

"I hear people died." He says it again, like a secret. Or maybe a challenge. Who here will dare to say that Derek Anderson is wrong?

Yongwon steps forward. "That's not true. The news said that only buildings were damaged. Buildings and trees."

Derek snorts. "Do you believe everything you hear on the news? It's all over the Internet, man. People died. They just don't want you to know."

I am with Yongwon. People write loads of crap on the Internet about everything. The news said everyone was evacuated in time. And, I mean — this is Canada. We are a civilized country. Our government wouldn't let people just die in a forest fire. Right?

Anyway, I keep my mouth shut. Maybe Yongwon can get away with challenging Derek. I am not so sure that I can.

Three bell tones ring somewhere over our heads. The speakers crackle, then the voice of our principal, Ms. Taylor, takes over. "Good morning, boys and girls. Please move to the gym for a special assembly."

Some of the guys groan. I'm not sure why. We have double social studies this morning. We were supposed to have a test. I'm hoping the assembly will go on for a while.

The basketball guys and I are the first ones in the gym. Derek and Yongwon lead the way straight to the back of the bleacher seats. Soon, the bleachers in front of us start to fill up.

Normally when our school has assemblies like this, it is total chaos. Students get into shoving matches over seats. Teachers begin shouting. Phones get confiscated. People end up in detention. But today, there is none of that. Here and there, students turn and whisper to friends. Phones remain in pockets. It is quiet enough that I can hear Ms. Taylor's high heels click-clack across the gym floor.

She stands in front of the microphone, looking around at all of us.

"Thank you for joining me here today," she begins. "I am sorry for disrupting your lessons. We teachers thought it was important to speak to you first thing this morning. As a school, we need to decide how to respond to the tragedy on the west coast of Vancouver Island."

I am surprised to hear the word *tragedy*. Usually you only hear that word when somebody dies. Or when a whole lot of people die far away. The palms of my hands feel clammy. The girls in front of me shift uneasily in their bleacher seats.

Ms. Taylor continues. "Now, I know you all have been checking the news. So you probably know most of the same information we do. But there will be rumours floating around school and on the Internet about the disaster. It is important to stick to the facts. And so we want to be clear. As of this morning at seven o'clock, fire crews in the affected areas have declared that the fires are now under control. No deaths or serious injuries have been reported."

The whole school seems to exhale at once. I take a few long deep breaths. To my left, Derek is shaking his head.

"However," says Ms. Taylor. "This *is* a tragedy. Many people have lost their homes, their businesses, their schools — everything. They are going to need our help. The school will be gathering non-perishable food items as well as old clothing and blankets to send to the affected communities. I encourage you all to come to us with your ideas as well, especially ideas for helping other young people. It has always been our duty as a school to assist those less fortunate than us. I know many of you have previous experience raising money and gathering items to send overseas to places like Afghanistan and Syria. This time, the people who need your help are much, much closer to home."

With that, she steps away from the microphone. The assembly is over. It's time to head back to class. I check my watch. Still almost an hour before recess. That might be enough time for our test.

"Did you study?" I ask Yongwon on our way out of the gym.

He gives me a look. "Is that supposed to be a joke?"

"There's a first time for everything."

"You know what Mr. Rossing is like," says Yongwon. "Any time something comes up in the news, we end up talking about it all class. It is really easy to distract him. There's no way we are doing that test today."

5 CANNED FOOD AND OLD CLOTHES

A big cardboard box sits on our kitchen table. It is packed with old jackets and mittens and woolly hats.

Dad returns from the basement carrying three pairs of winter boots.

"It will be getting cold soon," he says, shoving them into the box. "Those people are going to need lots of warm stuff."

"I'm going to be late for school, Dad."

At least this box is not too heavy. The other box was stuffed with canned food and packages of pasta and rice. It was like carrying concrete blocks. I could barely get it out to the driveway.

When Dad and I leave the house, Mom is just about to get into her car. She is dressed in a smart suit, the type she wears for trials at the courthouse. She takes one look at the box, then at Dad, then at me.

"More charity stuff for the fire relief efforts, eh?"

"Yeah," I say, a bit out of breath. "Even after yesterday, Dad managed to find more stuff in the basement."

Mom turns toward Dad. "Don't you think this is maybe a bit — much?"

Dad holds up his hands. "Too much? It's barely anything. Do you think we should make a quick run to the store before school?"

I look at him in disbelief. What is he trying to do to me? The other guys already made fun of me yesterday for showing up with boxes. I mean, everyone brought stuff in, but just odds and ends: a sweater here, a can of peas there. No one else has contributed the contents of their entire basement and most of the local supermarket.

Mom studies Dad's face. "All right. Well — have a good day, you two. Don't be late for class, Chris."

When Dad and I pull into the school parking lot, Greg Sparks is walking by.

"Hey, Sparky," I call out. "Come help us with this stuff."

His face lights up. "You got it, Big K."

"Big K?" says Dad, a grin spreading across his broad face. "So that's what they call you around here."

"No — it's not," I reply. I take out the last box and slam the door closed. "Thanks for the lift, Dad."

"You sure you don't need my help?"

"We'll be fine. See you at home."

I stagger up the stairs to the main building. My back aches. My arms feel like they are going to fall off.

"What's taking so long, Big K?" says Sparky from the top of the stairs. Seems like he got the clothing box. I would throw my box of food at him, if I could.

Inside school, Ms. Taylor is standing on the other side of the hallway. When she sees the boxes we are carrying, she walks toward us.

"What a wonderful contribution, Chris Khalili." She pronounces my name *Kai-lai-lai*.

I fake a smile. My arms hurt so much. I wonder if I will ever be able to use them again.

She points down the hallway. "Drop them off in the cafeteria, gentlemen. Same as yesterday."

Most of the cafeteria tables are already covered in boxes. I plunk down my box onto the first empty surface I see. Sparky places his next to mine. All around us, students are sorting and piling items.

"Look at all this stuff," says Sparky. "Our school's pretty generous, eh?"

I take a closer look at some of the stuff on the table in front of us. The place looks a bit like a garage sale — full of junk that people don't want.

"Would anyone actually wear this purple Christmas sweater?" I say. "Would anyone want to eat that jar of curry-flavoured pickled onions?"

Sparky looks at me like I just ruined his birthday. "Why do you have to be so harsh, man? People are giving this stuff away. They're just trying to help."

I remember the TV news. That house was on fire. Maybe the family who owned it really did lose everything. Maybe they would be thankful for pretty much anything. I'm not sure I would, though. I would have to be pretty hungry to eat curry-flavoured pickled onions. And you wouldn't get me into that Christmas sweater, no way. Not even if you burned up all my clothes.

Angeli and Helen, two of the prettiest girls in our grade, walk by. Angeli smiles at me. I am sure glad she can't read my thoughts. What kind of person would she think I am?

"Those boxes look great, guys," says Helen.

Sparky puffs up with pride like a fairground balloon. "It — it was nothing."

What a little punk. These aren't even his boxes. But there is no way to say so without sounding childish or jealous.

"We'd better get to class, Sparky," I say.

The girls giggle when they hear his nickname. It's small revenge, but at least it's something.

"Okay, Big K," he says.

We are late for Social Studies class, but Mr. Rossing just waves us into our seats. He is one of those young easygoing teachers you can easily manipulate if you are clever. A couple of weeks ago, Yongwon got him talking about basketball. He completely forgot what he was going to teach us and we didn't have to learn anything.

"Hey," says Yongwon beside me. "Have you seen Derek? Is he at school today?"

"No idea," I say, shrugging my shoulders. In Mr.

Rossing's class, Derek usually sits at our table. Today, there is no sign of him.

"All right, everyone," Mr. Rossing calls out from the front of the classroom. "Let's get to work. You each have a big sheet of white paper on your group tables. At the centre of each, you will find a single word. Not just any word, though — a word that is controversial."

Yongwon sticks up his hand. "What does controversial mean again?"

"Controversial means something that people argue over," explains Mr. Rossing. "And so on your sheets I would like you to create a list of pros and a list of cons related to your word."

I turn back toward our group table.

"We were supposed to have a test last lesson," says Sparky. "Mr. Rossing told us it would be postponed until today. Do you think I should remind him?"

For a moment, I think Yongwon is going to leap across the table and strangle Sparky.

"Don't you dare!" he hisses. Then he calms himself. "After all, we need to discuss our — controversial word."

Sparky grabs the piece of paper and flips it over. *Charity* is written in large letters. He raises his hand. "Um — Mr. Rossing. I think there has been a mistake."

Frowning slightly, the teacher walks over to our table. He points at the word. "Yes, that's right — charity. There's no mistake."

"But how are we supposed to fill in the Cons side of our paper?" asks Sparky. "Charity's a good thing."

Yongwon snorts. "Not necessarily. My dad always says that giving people things makes them lazy."

"That's just stupid," says Sparky.

"It's not stupid," says Yongwon. "Think about school. If we were all given As, we wouldn't be motivated to work."

"We're not talking about giving people luxury stuff," says Sparky. "Charity goes to poor people. It gives them the things that they need."

"This sounds pretty controversial to me," says Mr. Rossing with a knowing look. He glides away to another group.

Sparky jumps right back in. "I can't believe you don't get this. It's just people helping other people."

"Ah, come on," says Yongwon. "People don't give to charity because they really care about other people. They do it to feel better about themselves. To brag to their friends. To impress girls."

Sparky's face begins to turn red. "Even if that were true – and it's not – the people who get the stuff would still be grateful."

Yongwon shakes his head. "Are you even listening to yourself? Can you imagine what it feels like to be given other people's leftovers?"

My mind drifts away from the classroom to the piles of stuff on the tables in the cafeteria. What would it feel like to get a box of things like that? And then I think of my dad. Maybe he has been going overboard with the donations, but he does seem to actually care about the people who lost their homes in the fires. And at least his boxes are full of food people would actually eat and clothes they would actually wear. But could Yongwon be right? Could Dad really be doing all this just to feel better about himself?

I am starting to wonder if the debate between Yongwon and Sparky is going to be settled with fists when Derek enters the classroom. He hands Mr. Rossing a note.

"Hey, losers," he says, sitting down next to Yongwon. "What's going on?"

Yongwon points at Sparky. "He was just trying to tell us that people in poor countries would be happy to get his old T-shirts."

"It's not just poor countries," says Sparky. "Think about what happened right here on Vancouver Island. Those people need our help too. And I bet they do appreciate it."

"Well," says Derek. "You can ask them when they get here."

Sparky is about to argue with Yongwon again, but turns toward Derek instead. "Wait — what are you talking about?"

"You mean you guys haven't heard?" says Derek. He looks at us like we are kindergarten students.

"Everyone's talking about it online. They're coming here. To *our* school."

"Who?" says Yongwon.

Derek leans forward. "Kids whose houses got burned in the fire. And guess what —" He looks around at us, enjoying the suspense. "They're Indians," he says. "You know — like we studied back in Grade 5. Longhouses and totem poles and all that stuff."

"I don't think they like being called Indians," says Sparky.

A sneer descends onto Derek's face. "Hey — they are coming to my school. I'll call them whatever I want."

6 THE PEOPLE IN THE PARK

They are after me again, whooping and screaming and gnashing their teeth.

Faster, faster — you've got to go faster.

But they are different this time. They are on horseback, waving tomahawks in the air. As they close in on me, I can see the feathers in their hair and the war paint on their cheeks.

I am running as fast as I can. But there is no way I can run fast enough.

"Chris! Chris!" a voice calls out.

I wake up flustered and sweaty, all tangled in my blankets. Lucy is standing in the middle of my bedroom. In her white pyjamas, she looks like a tiny nurse.

"Are you okay, Chris?"

I wipe the back of my hand across my face. "Yeah, sure. Just a bad dream."

"Wh-what was it about?"

"Uh — I can't really remember," I tell her. That is not true. I just don't want to remember. That dream.

Man. It was like one of those old black-and-white cowboy-and-Indian shoot-em-up Westerns. The ones where the Indians are always the bad guys. I don't want to think about what kind of person that makes me, even if it was just a dream. One thing I do know is that I will never tell anyone about it. Not Lucy, not my parents — no one.

That is when I notice that Lucy is holding my running shoes.

"You said you were gonna run last night," she says. "But you didn't. Don't you want to win the race?"

I sit up groggily. Lucy shoves the shoes onto my lap.

"Whoa," I say. "Ease up, Coach. Can I at least change out of my pyjamas first?"

She might be only six, but she is right. Coach Clark sent an email out last night saying that the qualifiers have been rescheduled to this Friday. That gives me just five days to train and get ready. So, even though every muscle in my body screams at me to stay in bed, I stagger to my feet. Once Lucy is out of the room, I pull on a pair of shorts and an old T-shirt.

When I get downstairs, Dad is folding laundry in the living room.

"Morning, Chris," he says.

"Hey, Dad." I shove my feet into my shoes. "Off for a run!"

"What about breakfast?" he calls after me. But I am already out the front door.

Dad is a guy who believes in breakfast before anything. If Victoria was ever attacked in the morning, Dad would be doomed. He would be in the kitchen making bacon and eggs instead of racing for the bomb shelter with everyone else.

Outside, Sunday morning in Victoria is cool but there is not a cloud in the sky. I decide to run along Beach Drive, one of my favourite routes. It starts near the university, and continues down along the seashore all the way to Trafalgar Park. The park is on a point that juts out into the sea. Today, the air is so clear that I can see a snow-capped peak across the water. That is Mount Baker, all the way down in the United States.

When the breeze is behind you, running is like flying. You glide on the wind like a soaring eagle, skimming across the earth. Nothing can slow you down.

Nothing except Sunday joggers, that is. As I cut back toward town, I run into a pair of them. With their butts like waddling rhinos, they block the entire sidewalk. To get around them, I have to step out onto the road. A horn honks loudly behind me. Spooked, I jump back up onto the curb. As I run on, a bus zooms past.

Once, a few years ago, Dad asked me if I was going jogging. That was when I was just starting to get serious about running. I told him that jogging is what fat old people do. I never jog. I run.

With the golf course on my right, I continue along Foul Bay Road. This is where I hit the wall. I don't know why. It is as if the wings I had by the seaside have transformed into parachutes. My legs grow heavier and heavier as the gentle climb transforms into a steep slope. Maybe I ran the first part too fast or got put off my stride by that bus. Maybe my Dad was right. Maybe I should have had breakfast first.

Come on, I tell myself. *What if this happens in the race? You need to push yourself. You need to go faster.*

But it does not work. The hill keeps getting steeper, and my legs keep getting heavier.

That's when the dream returns. Horses, feathers, war paint, tomahawks. Bloodthirsty savages whooping and screaming and gnashing their teeth.

Faster, faster — you've got to go faster.

I try to think of something else to run away from. Anything else. But the Indians won't get out of my head. And soon I am running hard again, powering up the hill. Running for my life.

The top of the hill arrives so quickly that it surprises my feet. They slam down on the level ground, still expecting an incline. My legs go rubbery. But with a few quick strides, I regain my rhythm and I am on my way again. Less than one kilometre to go. That's like the last lap of a race. Now is no time to slow down.

Cavendish Park is on the same street as my house. There is a black metal lamppost at the edge of the park that is always my finish line. And so today, as always, when the lamppost appears up ahead, I know that it is time to go, go, go. But it is not enough to have a destination. I need to be chased. And so the bloodthirsty savages appear again, this time right on my heels.

I strain every muscle all the way to the lamppost. I have to push right through to the finish line. Often, the final stretch is where the race is won or lost.

And — done! I slow to a trot, then a walk, wandering out onto the soft green grass of Cavendish Park. My legs feel wobbly, like jellyfish arms. I drink the air in long sips, trying to regain my breath as my lungs heave up and down.

"Hey, there — you all right?"

Standing in front of me are a tall guy and a small dog. The guy is wearing blue jeans and a dark grey jacket with crossed hockey sticks on the sleeves. It is obvious from his face that he is a high school kid like me, but he is big enough to be a man. And though I have never actually met one before, there is no question about one thing.

This guy is an Indian. I mean First Nations. I mean —

"My name's Jason," he says. "You live on this block?"

"Y-yeah," I stammer, still trying to catch my breath. "I'm Chris."

He nods, then looks at me strangely. "Hey, were you being chased by someone just now?"

I feel a bit sick to my stomach. Jason seems like a cool enough guy. What if he knew what was just running through my mind? I mean — come on. Tomahawks? Feathers? War paint? Whooping and screaming on top of horses?

I shake my head. "Nah — of course not."

He points behind me. "Glad to hear it. You kept looking over your shoulder. I thought you might be running from the cops."

There is an awkward pause.

"I'm just training," I tell him. "I run for Oak Bay."

"Oak Bay?" Suddenly he looks interested. "You mean the school?"

"Yeah."

"No way!" he exclaims. "That's where we're gonna be going to school, starting this week — my sister and I."

On the far side of the park there are three rectangular structures. I call them *structures* because they are not houses. They look like *motorhomes* — those things that people go camping in. But where did they come from? And why are they here?

I point at the sleeve of Jason's jacket. "So — you're a hockey player?"

"Yeah," he says, looking down at the ground. "Well — I was, before our hockey rink burned down."

Of course. How stupid am I? These are the people who everyone has been talking about. Jason, his sister, and the rest of his family are here because of the forest fires.

My stomach growls.

"Hey, listen," I tell him. "I'm starving. I've got to go home and get some breakfast. But if you want — we can walk to school tomorrow."

He shrugs. "That would be good. If you don't, I'll probably get lost. This city is huge."

That makes me chuckle. Vancouver is a big city. Montreal is a big city. But Victoria —?

"All right," I tell him. "See you tomorrow morning."

7 NEW KID

When I come down from my room the next morning, Sarah and Lucy are side-by-side at the kitchen table. They scrabble madly with their knives and forks. Golden waffles dripping in maple syrup fly into their mouths at an astonishing speed.

"Morning, girls."

Neither of them even pauses to look at me.

"Here you go, Chris," says Dad. He hands me my own plate of waffles. They smell amazing. Sitting down next to my sisters, I tuck right in.

"You three eat like farm animals," says Dad.

He is wearing a big black T-shirt. The words *I am your father* are written across his belly. The *I* is a picture of a red lightsaber.

"Dad," I say. "Please tell me you're not planning to wear that shirt outside."

He shrugs. "Why not? I am proud to be a father. Do you want a lift to school today?"

"No, no, no — that's okay," I reply. "Actually, I'm

walking to school with a new kid, Jason. You know, the guy whose family is — living in the park."

"Ah," says Dad. "Yes. The refugees."

It's easy to forget sometimes that English is not my dad's first language. I am so used to his accent that it barely even crosses my mind. Now and then, though, he chooses a word that is not quite right. *Refugees* are people who come here from other countries, fleeing wars and dictators and poverty. People from Canada can't be refugees. Right?

Mom rushes into the kitchen, her laptop bag clutched under one arm. Grabbing a single waffle from a plate on the counter, she kisses Dad on the cheek.

"Busy day?" he asks her.

Mom sighs. "You can say that again."

Dad lays a hand on her arm. "Chris was just telling me that he is going to show a new boy around. You know — from one of the families staying in the park? The Indians. Isn't that a noble thing to do?"

Mom cringes a little when he says the word *Indians*.

"Yes," she agrees. "While they are here, we should be kind to them."

Mom is a lawyer. She spends lots of time fighting in court to help homeless people and poor people. And so her lack of enthusiasm surprises me a little. But before I can think much about this, she is already out the door.

"I'd better get going too," I announce, standing up from the table. "Great breakfast, Dad. Thanks a lot.

Remember to take that shirt off if you leave the house."

He looks at me. "So — you're telling me to go outside with no shirt on?"

"Yuck!" says Lucy, which makes my dad laugh pretty hard.

"Hey," he says to me, taking a plastic bag out of the fridge. "Don't forget your lunch."

At the far end of Cavendish Park, I see a man next to the lamppost. It is not until I am standing right next to him that I realize it is Jason. He is a really big dude.

"Hey," I say. "Ready for your first day?"

He looks back at the motorhomes in the park. "Yeah — I guess. My parents already took my sister to school. They wanted me to come along. I told them I was going to wait here for someone who knows his way around. So — yeah, thanks, man. You saved me from showing up to my first day with my parents and my little sister."

Dad's *I am your father* T-shirt swishes through my mind.

It seems that Jason likes to move quickly, even when walking to school. We hurry past the drugstore, the aquatic centre, and a retirement home. It is a good thing that my legs have finally loosened up, after that hard run yesterday.

"There are so many old people here in Victoria," says Jason, as we pass a second retirement home.

"You've got that right," I agree. "Last week, on

the bus, I was the only person without grey hair."

It is quite warm today. When we get to school, the playing fields are full of students.

"Come on," I say to Jason. "I'll introduce you to some of the guys."

Yongwon, Sparky, Derek, and a few others are joking around by one of the soccer goals. When they see the two of us coming over, their chatter dies down. They all turn to look at the new kid.

"Hey, guys," I say, trying to sound as casual as possible. "This is Jason."

Nobody says anything for what seems like a very long time. Jason stands there with his hands in his pockets. They look at him. He looks at them.

"Wow," says Yongwon, at last. "You're a real —"

I feel my throat tighten.

"— hockey player?"

Jason points to the crossed hockey sticks on his jacket sleeve. "Yeah — back home our band has a pretty good hockey team. Or at least we did."

Yongwon nods approvingly. "You were in a band too? Cool. What kind of music did you play?"

Everyone turns toward Jason. The guy is huge. He could crush Yongwon without even straining a muscle. Instead, he smiles politely. "Not that kind of band. Our band is a member of the Nuu-chah-nulth nation. Most white people call us the Nootka."

"What do Koreans call you?" asks Yongwon.

"Uh — I'm not sure," says Jason. "Don't think I've ever met a Korean before. There aren't too many of them on the reserve."

"We keep asking Yongwon if he's a South Korean or a North Korean," says Sparky. "But he never gives us a straight answer."

Yongwon raises an eyebrow. "Maybe I'm a spy, Sparky."

"Aren't spies supposed to be clever?" asks Derek.

Yongwon shrugs off the insult. "Maybe I'm just pretending to be a dumb jock, man. Could be a great disguise for a spy."

Jason laughs at that. His shoulders are hanging loose now, and his body leans comfortably to one side. The six of us are standing roughly in a circle, with no one left out. Everyone seems pretty relaxed. But then, I notice Derek. Eyes narrowed, jaw thrust forward — he is glaring at Jason like he stares down other teams in basketball.

My thoughts are interrupted by a woman's voice. "Excuse me — would you happen to be Jason Thomas?"

Ms. Taylor is standing next to us in the grass, high heels and all.

"Um — yeah," says Jason. "I guess I am."

She smiles in that official teacher way. "It's time for your orientation. The rest of the new students are over by the front entrance, including your sister. They arrived together. What happened to you?"

Jason opens his mouth, but can't seem to find the right words.

"He walked to school with me," I tell her.

Another official smile, this time in my direction. "Ah — well, that was very good of you, Chris. Follow me, please, Jason."

That was good of you, Chris. Why did she have to say it that way? I only offered to walk to school with Jason because he seemed like an okay guy. And we were coming from the same direction. It wasn't charity. I don't need a pat on the back.

Yongwon watches the two of them walk away. "Jason seems cool enough. Even if he doesn't know much about Korea."

"Probably knows more than you know about where he comes from," I say. "Name one fact about the Nuu-chah-nulth."

Yongwon thinks hard for a moment. "Don't they ride horses or something? And wear feathers on their heads? And live in teepees?"

I hold up my hands. "Those are the Native people who live on the prairies. And I am pretty sure they don't do that stuff very much anymore either."

I feel pretty good about myself for a moment. My class did a project on the Nuu-chah-nulth back in Grade 5, though my teacher called them the Nootka. We made model longhouses and totem poles and everything.

Derek steps forward. "My dad says Indians are all the same. They're freeloaders. They're lazy. They don't work. Our government gives them everything, but they spend all their money on alcohol and stuff like that."

"Well," says Yongwon, though he sounds far from certain. "I have heard people say that."

Anger rises in my throat. "Just because your dad says something, Derek, it doesn't mean it's true."

Derek's face flushes red. "What, and what *you* say is always right? Who do you think you are, Chris? You're not better than the rest of us."

I expect at least one of my friends to come to my defence, but no one does. Not even Yongwon. They all just look away. When the bell goes, Derek steps in front of me and snorts in my face. The other guys follow him into the school.

I'm in the right, I tell myself. But deep down, I remember what ran through my mind during training on Sunday. Those savages waving tomahawks were exactly what Yongwon had in mind. So what does that make me? Am I really any different from Derek?

8 FUN RUN

On Thursday morning, Angeli and Helen find me before class.

"Hey, Chris," says Angeli. "We really need your help with something."

Her eyelashes flutter up and down. When do girls learn how to do that? And why does it make me want to agree to do anything she asks?

"We organized an event for after school today," says Helen. She does the eyelash-flutter too, but it doesn't have quite the same effect. "It's to help welcome the new students. You know, the ones — from up north."

I nod eagerly. "Yeah — I mean, of course. No problem. What is it?"

Angeli smiles. "It's exactly your kind of thing. It's a Fun Run! You really haven't heard about it already?"

"Um," I say. A Fun Run. That is so not my kind of thing. I don't run for fun. I run to win.

Helen jumps in again. "The Fun Run will be one lap of the Jungle trail. Coach Clark says all of the new kids need buddies to run alongside so they don't get lost. She told us you are good friends with that guy Jason —"

Good friends? That seems like an exaggeration. We walked to school together on Monday. But we don't have any of the same classes. I have barely seen the guy since.

"Look," I tell the girls. "I'm sorry, but I've got a really big race tomorrow. I can't run today. You can even ask Coach Clark."

Helen glares at me, steel in her eyes. "Fine. We'll have a much better Fun Run without you anyway."

Angeli just looks down at the gym floor.

"I–I'm sorry," I splutter.

But they are already moving away.

For the rest of the day, I try to put the Fun Run out of my mind. This is easier said than done. Apparently I am the last kid in school — maybe the last kid on Earth — to hear about it. There are posters up all over school: hallways, classrooms, bathrooms. Online, when I go back through people's posts from this week, there are tons about the Fun Run. How did I miss this? I really don't know. Maybe there has just been so much stuff about the fire and the new kids that I sort of stopped paying attention. My focus has been on getting ready for the qualifiers. That probably makes me sound like a bad person. But it is the truth.

I don't think about the Fun Run again until my last class of the day: PE. We are supposed to be playing badminton. Yongwon and I are using our rackets as guitars.

"Yongwon!" I hiss when I see Coach Clark heading our way. We're not supposed to be goofing around with the gym equipment.

"Chris, can I speak to you for a moment?" says Coach Clark.

"It was Yongwon's fault —"

"Never mind that," she says. "Just — come chat with me for a second."

She leads me over to the far side of the gym. "Chris — I need you to help with the Fun Run today."

Something strange is going on here. Coach Clark is usually so enthusiastic about everything. Right now, it sounds like someone is standing behind her, holding a sword to her ribs.

"But the qualifiers are tomorrow," I protest.

She sighs. "Chris — I know, I know. I tried everything to get you and the other cross-country runners out of it. But I've been told to make it happen. I'm afraid I have no choice."

I have a pretty good theory about who told her to make this happen. This has Ms. Taylor's fingerprints all over it. No one else could put Coach Clark under so much pressure.

"You can just jog it," she tells me. "You know — take it easy. Chris, will you do it — please? It would really help me out of a jam, mate. And I am sure that your new friend Jason would appreciate it."

I nod my head slowly. What choice do I have? It would be a jerk move now in every way to say no. But the whole thing is so unfair. Ms. Taylor would never make the basketball team play a charity match the day before a tournament. Why are we runners any different? It's not like the basketball team wins any more than we do.

After school, I find Jason out on the playing fields. A girl is standing next to him.

"Hey," he says to me. "This is my sister, Anna."

The new kids — there are eleven altogether — are standing nearby. They have matching red shirts with *Nuu-chah-nulth* printed in white letters on the front. Two or three are wearing jeans. They do not look too excited about the Fun Run.

Along with the red shirt, Jason is wearing a pair of black shorts that hang well below his knees. On his feet are a pair of floppy grey sneakers. They look like they have been worn for at least a hundred years.

He grimaces. "Man — I'd give anything to have my old shoes back. The ones I had before the fire."

Yongwon comes toward us in a ridiculous costume. It is some sort of dinosaur onesie, the yellow kind with a zipper up the front. Looking around, I see that he is not the only one.

"What are you doing?" I ask.

"Nice costume, Yongwon," says a girl's voice behind us. We turn around. Helen. Well — that explains a lot.

Angeli is beside her. She waves at Jason. "Hey, how are the shirts? Is the design okay? My older brother knows a guy, so we got them printed extra fast."

"Um — yeah, they are really cool," mumbles Jason.

"What is that, anyway?" I ask him, after the girls have gone. Above *Nuu-chah-nulth* is a piece of First Nations art. It looks like something you might see in a museum. I think it's a bear, but it could be a man with big ears.

Jason shrugs. "I don't know, man. That girl asked us to wear these shirts to promote — uh — *our* culture. But it's not our people's art. It might be Inuit — you know, like, from the Arctic. To be honest, I'm not really sure."

My mouth falls open. "What? That's so embarrassing! Why didn't you tell her?"

He shrugs. "Hey — she tried. I don't want to make her feel bad. Plus — she's kinda cute."

A whistle sounds behind us.

"Line up, everyone!" calls out Coach Clark. "The Fun Run's about to begin. Boys, you're up first."

Yongwon makes a face as we approach the start line. "Seriously — Fun Run? It's like one of those opposite things we learned in English — what was that called, a metaphor?"

"An oxymoron," says Jason.

"Yeah, Yongwon," I say. "You moron."

Jason lines up alongside me. "I heard you're my running buddy."

"Yeah," I reply. "We are supposed to stick together." What I don't tell him is that I never run for fun. I run to win, every time. I can't run any other way.

The whistle blows again. Fifty boys surge forward, all elbows and shoulders. I push my way straight to the front of the crowd. But then I remember Jason. Fighting every racing instinct, I cut back on my speed. Five guys zoom past me, including Sparky and Yongwon.

A bright red shirt appears alongside me.

"Good start," says Jason. "Why did you slow down?"

He isn't huffing or puffing. He seems to be running quite comfortably.

"It's all good," I say. Actually, getting passed by Yongwon and Sparky felt about as good as getting stabbed in the knee with a fork.

We run side by side for a while, feet pounding the ground as it rises and falls. I can still see Yongwon and Sparky and the other three guys. They aren't too far ahead of us — yet.

Another runner slips past on my right side. My teeth clench. I don't know how much more of this I can take.

"Hey," says Jason, nudging me with his elbow. "What are you doing? Go for it. I won't say anything to Coach Clark."

He does not have to tell me twice. My legs shift into overdrive. I zoom between the first two runners. I make

Fun Run

Yongwon and Sparky look like they are standing still.

Pretty soon, I am all alone, out in front. Students and teachers are cheering from all sides.

"Look at him go!"

"Come on, Chris!"

The finish line appears ahead of me. From habit, I take a quick look over my shoulder. That is when I see Jason. His big tree-trunk legs are pumping up and down like pistons. His nostrils puff out air like a charging bull. He is closing on me, fast.

Shocked, I take off toward the finish line. And then, in my mind, I see the last thing I want to see. Bloodthirsty savages waving tomahawks, throwing spears, screaming for my blood.

I cross the finish line in first place.

"Great race," says Jason, sticking out his hand. I grasp it firmly. He is gasping, trying to catch his breath. "I almost got you. But it was like you were running for your life."

"Nah," I tell him, looking away. "It was just for fun. Just a fun run."

9 A BOTTLE OF WHISKEY, A CARTON OF EGGS

"Lucy, Sarah, Chris — dinnertime!"

That Fun Run took something out of me. I go down the stairs one at a time. My sisters push past me on their way to the table.

"Hurry up, gramps," says Lucy.

"Yeah, old man," adds Sarah.

They cackle together, like little witches.

Yup, that's me — big winner of the Oak Bay Fun Run. Beaten to the dinner table by my little sisters.

"You okay, Chris?" asks Dad, watching as I lower myself into a chair. "You are moving a bit slowly."

"Nah, I'm fine," I tell him, though it feels like I am ninety years old.

The plate in front of me fills with a mountain of saffron rice. The lamb is soft and juicy. The vegetables have been marinated in a delicious sauce. There is thick white yogurt for dipping. And of course, as always, there is warm flatbread.

"You look like a new man, Chris," says Dad, when

A Bottle of Whiskey, A Carton of Eggs

I have finished eating.

He might be right. I feel like a teenager again, though a pretty sleepy teenager.

"When's Mommy coming home?" asks Lucy.

Dad pulls his phone out of his pocket. "She just texted me. She should be back soon."

Looking at my dad, I wonder if he is happy with his life. Sure, it is not the old days anymore, when all men worked and all women stayed home. There are even other kids at school who have stay-at-home dads. And it is nice to have someone around when I get home from school. Mom could never do that. Sure, Dad worries too much about my blisters and unfinished homework. But his cooking sure is fantastic.

Sometimes, though, I wonder if staying home and looking after kids is what Dad always wanted. Was there ever something that he loved to do as much as I love running? Something that made his heart race? Something that he really cared about?

He stands up from the table. "Everyone get enough to eat? Anyone need seconds?"

I pat my stomach. "I'm stuffed."

"Food was okay?"

I take a deep breath. "Delicious. You should open a restaurant, Dad."

He laughs. "I would make the whole city fat."

From behind us comes the sound of the front door opening and closing.

"Mommy!" shouts Lucy. She and Sarah leap from their seats and charge out of the room. They return dragging Mom along by both hands. Mom looks like someone who has been lost in the desert for a week. I wonder what kind of day at work could do that to a person.

She pats both of my sisters on their heads, then slumps down into a chair. A plate full of food appears in front of her.

"Thank you so much, honey," she says to my dad, sending a tired smile his way.

Lucy and Sarah begin creeping toward the stairs.

"Not so fast, girls," says Dad. "Clear the table first, please."

Lucy's lips form into a pout. "But we cleared the table *last* night."

"Yeah," Sarah protests. "It's Chris's turn."

"You're right," says Dad. "But Chris and I are going to be busy tonight. Can my best two little helpers please take care of the dishes?"

Sarah glares at him. Lucy just sighs. Together, they trudge off to the kitchen. They look like they have been assigned to work in a coal mine.

Mom glances up from her food. "What are you two guys so busy with tonight?"

I look over at Dad. I've got no idea what he is up to.

He looks down at the ground. "I — I've gathered together some stuff for the people in the park.

Nothing fancy — just a few nice things. I thought Chris could help me take them over tonight. You've been hanging out with one of the boys, right, Chris? What's his name?"

"Jason," I say through my teeth. "Jason Thomas."

Dad frowns at me. "Are you sure that's his name?"

I don't really know what to say. What is he talking about? Why would Jason tell me a fake name?

"I thought those people all had names like Jason Running Wolf or Jason Eagle Feathers," says Dad.

Mom holds up a hand. "Whoa, whoa, whoa. I think names like those are only found on the prairies, in places like Alberta and Saskatchewan. And they aren't even all that common there anymore. But are you sure it's a good idea to take stuff to them? You don't know them, Al."

Al is my dad's name. Well — that's what everyone calls him, even Mom. His full name is Alireza.

His chest puffs out a few inches. "Of course it's a good idea. Think of everything these poor people must have gone through."

Mom closes her eyes, then sighs. "Fine. It's up to you. Just don't be surprised if they aren't thrilled to see you. Not everyone likes gifts they aren't expecting."

What does she mean? Surely everyone likes gifts, especially ones they aren't expecting. Why is Mom so against this?

Dad rolls his eyes. "You worry too much. Everything will be fine."

A few minutes later, we are walking toward Cavendish Park. Plastic bags full of rice and chicken soup and pasta sauce are dangling from my hands. Dad marches alongside, carrying more bags. I am still not sure why Mom was against this. All I know is that I don't want to be here. Is Dad out of his mind? This is going to be beyond embarrassing.

Only the shadowy outlines of the motorhomes are visible in the fading daylight. In the one nearest to us, there is a light on in the front window.

"That's Jason's place," I tell Dad.

He nods. "Okay."

The front steps of the motorhome are aluminum. They shudder a little under his weight. Two knocks on the door produce a rattling sound, followed by a dog barking inside. I stand back, wishing that this could all just be over.

A man's face appears in the doorway. It is the first time I have seen him, but it is obvious he is Jason's father. Looking at him feels like travelling forward in a time machine and visiting Jason in the future. Except for a few flecks of grey in his hair, the two of them could be brothers.

"Can I help you?" he asks. He doesn't open the screen door.

Dad holds up the plastic bags. "Good evening. My

name is Alireza Khalili. My family lives just a little way down the road. We wanted to bring you some groceries to help you get settled in, especially after all that you have been through."

The man stares back at him. "Thank you, but we are doing just fine. Maybe you should save your canned soup for your own kids."

Dad takes a bottle of amber liquid out of one of the shopping bags. "I've got whiskey. The good stuff. Not the cheap rubbish."

The man's lip curls upward. "We don't allow alcohol in this — house."

Just then, Jason appears behind him in the doorway.

"Dad," he says, gesturing toward us. "What are you doing? This is my friend Chris from school."

He pushes past his father and opens the screen door. "I'm sorry. Please — come in. Let me take those from you."

He reaches out to my dad and receives the grocery bags. Dad waves a hand at me. Reluctantly I step forward. Jason's father takes the bags out of my hands and disappears into the back of the motorhome. Somewhere inside, a girl is crying and a woman is trying to calm her down.

"Look — I'm sorry," says Jason, in a low voice. "My dad's not usually like this. We've had a rough night. Some kids came by and threw eggs."

I suddenly notice the star-shaped spatters of liquid all

over the side of the motorhome. I can see bits of white shell in them. It makes me feel sick to my stomach.

Jason looks down. "The eggs were nothing. What they yelled at us was worse. They called us freeloaders. They said the government gives us everything, we don't pay taxes, don't pay for university. They called us druggies and alcoholics. And they said we should get out of Victoria and go back to where we came from."

Jason's father returns to the doorway. He is not smiling — far from it — but the expression on his face has softened a little.

"I'm so sorry," says my dad, tucking the whiskey bottle into his jacket pocket. "I truly am."

My dad is quiet as we walk together back through the park. And at first, it is too dark to see his face. But then we pass a streetlight, and I see his eyes and the faintest glimmer of tears.

10 WORN-OUT SNEAKERS

"Why are you walking like a pirate?" asks Yongwon the next morning at school. "Are you planning to audition for the school play?"

"Shut up," I tell him. I start running up the steps just to prove I am fine. But every muscle in my body complains and I have to stop before I reach the top. "It's probably just a cramp or something. Stupid Fun Run yesterday."

"Haven't you got some other race today?"

I nod. "Yeah — it's the qualifiers for the city final!"

Yongwon lets out a long low whistle. "Hope you're not too tired to run."

"I'm never too tired to run," I tell him. "And never too tired to win either."

The math classroom is empty, so we sit right at the back. That is when I tell Yongwon about what happened the night before in Cavendish Park. I don't bring up the groceries that we carried over or the tears in my dad's eyes. But I do tell him about the eggs and the insults that were hurled at Jason's place.

"That's horrible," says Yongwon. "They've already been through so much. And now some idiots go and do that."

"I know. It makes me feel ashamed of Victoria."

Yongwon shakes his head. "Nah — there are people like that everywhere. At my elementary school back in South Korea, we had a few kids whose families had escaped from North Korea."

"There were North Korean refugees in your school?" I exclaim. "You never told me that."

"Yeah. It was really hard for them. They didn't understand how anything worked in South Korea. Most people were nice and tried to help them out. But there were a few kids at school who were pretty brutal. They called them enemies or spies or said their parents had come to steal our parents' jobs."

"Did you ever think about doing anything about it?" I ask him. "What about telling the tough kids to shut their fat mouths?"

Yongwon shakes his head. "Maybe I should have. But it was easier to just stay quiet, you know? They were really mean kids. I am ashamed to say it, but I was just glad they weren't picking on me."

"Well — if I find out who egged Jason's place," I tell him, "they're toast."

He laughs bitterly. "Eggs and toast."

"That's not funny, Yongwon."

"It's a bit funny," he says.

"Yeah, I guess you're right."

Yongwon thinks for a moment. "There's one more thing I remember about it. My mom always said that the kids who bullied the North Koreans had learned that kind of thing from their parents. So yeah — it is the kid's fault. But the parents are part of the problem too."

Yongwon always calls himself a dumb jock. Most of the time, he plays that part pretty well. But he isn't one. Forget grades. Yongwon is actually a pretty smart guy.

In math class, equations, fractions, square roots, and variables swirl around me. There is no room in my head for anything right now except for the race after school. Well — that and what happened to Jason and his family. I spend French and Social Studies staring out the window at the dull grey sky. After lunch, the rain starts drizzling down. My thoughts turn toward muddy slopes and slippery tree roots. Could be a tough race today.

We finish the day with Science class, which starts with a bang. Mr. Midgley fills a balloon with some kind of gas. He holds a match to it. There is a loud whoosh and the balloon disappears in a ball of flame. The whole class bursts into applause. But then it turns out that we have to learn something about this explosion. Numbers and notes go up on the board, and my mind goes out the window.

Finally, the bell rings.

Mr. Midgley walks to the front of the class. He says something about our homework assignment but all I hear is "*Blah, blah,* and *blah.*"

The only thing I can think about is the white minibus that I know will be waiting outside school, ready to take us to the race. And sure enough, when I get outside, it is there.

"Come on, everyone — hurry up!" shouts Coach Clark. "We need to get there in time to warm up."

Inside the minibus, someone calls my name. "Hey, Chris — come sit over here."

I can't believe my eyes. It's Jason. He's in one of the seats at the back.

"Hey," I say, sitting down next to him. "What are you doing here?"

He shrugs. "After the Fun Run yesterday, Coach Clark suggested that I should join the cross-country team. I haven't been able to get into any hockey here yet. So I thought, why not? I've never liked running much, but yesterday was actually kind of fun."

"Oh," I say. "Well — that's great."

Visions of yesterday's race invade my mind. Jason was right behind me. I still won, but it was closer than it should have been.

I try to shake off the memory. It was just a Fun Run, after all. Today is the real thing.

It is a short drive to the place where we will run. When we arrive, the minibus pulls into a small gravel parking lot. Its doors snap open.

"You've got fifteen minutes," calls out Coach Clark. "Go get warmed up."

Worn-Out Sneakers

The rain has eased a little, but the ground beneath my feet is soft and muddy. Bending down, I do my best to stretch out my tired legs.

Sparky comes over and stands next to me. There is still a bandage on his leg from his fall in the previous race. Jason joins us too. We do a bit of warm-up running, followed by more stretches. No one says anything. The time for chit-chat is over.

"Runners — to your marks!"

At the starting line, Sparky and Jason stand on my right. To my left is Rocket-Shoes, his mop of frizzy red hair tied up in a white headband. The Man in Black is there too, staring grimly at his own shoes.

"Ready —" shouts the starter, "— Set —"

I bend my knees, preparing for liftoff.

"— Go!"

Right off the start, two runners slip and fall over. Three more tumble on their way down the hill. I manage to hurdle over one guy who sprawls right in front of me. Jason and Sparky are not so lucky.

By the time I get to the bottom of the hill, half the runners have fallen on their butts or their faces. I race off toward the trees, opening up as big a lead as I can. I make sure to keep an eye on where I place my feet. This trail is as slippery as a skating rink.

As I hit the single-track through the trees, the rain disappears. Cool air rushes across my face. I take the straight stretches fast, the corners slower. I duck under low-hanging branches. I dodge around slippery flat stones.

At the start of my second lap, I slip and slide down the first downhill, fighting to keep my balance. Soon I am on the flats again, flying toward the forest. Entering the trees once more, I do a quick shoulder-check. No one in sight. I've got victory in my pocket, as long as I can stay on my feet.

The second lap seems to take no time at all. Coach Clark stands by the starting line, fists clenched. "Come on, Chris — one more lap!"

The rain picks up again. I scramble down the hill, shoes caked with mud. Feeling the pull of the finish line, I race into the trees one last time. But on the first corner, my left foot slips out from under me. I go down hard, landing in a heap on the side of the trail.

Come on, I tell myself. *Get up. You're way ahead. They can't catch you now.*

Staggering to my feet, I brush myself off and keep going. I push on and on until I break out of the trees. The final hill to the finish line appears. My legs are aching now. My lungs are burning. But I keep going.

Faster, faster — you've got to go faster.

The end is so close that I can almost taste it.

I don't notice the pounding footsteps until they are right behind me. With the effort of climbing the hill, I guess I just drowned everything out.

Worn-Out Sneakers

It could be Rocket-Shoes or the Man in Black or Sparky. It could even be a horde of wild Indians waving spears and tomahawks. I don't look back. I keep going. So I don't see who it is until I reach the top of the hill.

Jason.

He catches up to me just as the finish line appears ahead of us. He rumbles alongside me for a few strides. Then he surges into the lead. Mud flies up into the air, kicked up by his worn-out sneakers, as he crosses the finish line in first place.

11 BREAKING BREAD

"What an honour it will be for you to represent our school," says Ms. Taylor, catching me in the hallway between classes. "It's just wonderful. Three boys and two girls from Oak Bay Secondary at the city finals."

"Good job, Chris," says Angeli, smiling softly. "I heard it was a really close race."

"Did you let Jason beat you?" whispers Yongwon. "Come on — you can tell me."

At least it is finally Friday. I have been listening to this kind of stuff all week, and I am sick of it. I know it shouldn't bother me so much. Coach Clark said that the important thing was to qualify for the city finals. And Jason has been really good about everything. He is not the kind of guy to rub your face in a loss. So why can't I let it go? Why can't I stop thinking that if Jason had never come to this school, I would have won the race?

Sparky catches up with me in the cafeteria at lunchtime. He qualified for the city finals too, squeaking ahead of another runner to finish in eighth place.

"City finals coming up, Big K," he says. He plunks his cafeteria tray down next to mine.

Sparky has not stopped talking about the city finals all week. Every time he sees me or Jason, his face lights up and his babbling begins.

"I bet we're going to finish one-two-three!" he says, speaking with his mouth full of pasta.

"Sure, Sparky," I reply. "And pigs might fly over the moon."

What I can't say out loud is that I really don't care whether Sparky or Jason finish second or third or dead last. All I care about is crossing that finish line in first place.

For most of the week, Jason has been hanging out with us during lunchtime. Today, he is sitting with the rest of the Nuu-chah-nulth kids. The kids are all different ages, but they seem to know each other really well. They don't mix much with the rest of the students. Most of the time, they just stick together.

Derek gestures in their direction as he sits down at our table. "I told you. They don't belong here. They think they are special — better than the rest of us. They don't want to fit in."

Yongwon snorts. "Derek, who would even want to fit in with you? You're lucky we let you hang around with us."

"But my dad told me they should just try to —"

"No one cares what your stupid racist dad told you."

Face flushing red, Derek jumps to his feet. "What did you say to me?"

Yongwon keeps his eyes on his plate. "Sit down. Or else I'll say it again."

Derek glares at him. "You'd better watch it. I'll — I'll —"

His voice trails off. Fists clenched, he storms away.

Yongwon has not moved. Lifting his fork, he takes a bite of macaroni. "I don't like people being ignorant when I'm trying to eat lunch."

Looking around the cafeteria, I catch Jason glancing over at us. He is too far away to hear our conversation, but he can probably tell that something strange has just gone down. He nods in my direction. I nod back.

Guys around us come over to congratulate Yongwon. A few even pat him on the back.

"You're right, dude," says somebody behind me.

"You told him," says somebody else.

If Yongwon had stayed quiet, most of these guys would be agreeing with Derek right now. They are the kind of guys that always follow the crowd.

Yongwon's smile is cool and confident. Maybe I am the only person in the whole cafeteria who notices that the fork in his hand is shaking.

★★★

"This movie is boring," says Sarah. "Can we watch the other one?"

A magazine sits next to me on the couch, unread. My right thumb scrolls mindlessly through different screens on my phone.

"What's the difference?" I say without looking up. "Aren't they both about princesses anyway?"

Lucy snatches the phone out of my hand. "The other one is about *fairies*. Not wimpy pink fairies. Mean fairies. Spiky fairies. Fairies that rip off your ears."

"Okay, okay," I say, taking my phone back. "I'll put the other one on."

I can't believe this. It is a sunny Saturday afternoon, and I am stuck in front of the television with my sisters.

Good thing none of the guys from school can see me now. Chris and the spiky mean fairies. I might have to change schools. I might have to move to the United States.

From outside there is the sound of tires crunching on gravel. A car door opens and closes, followed by Dad's voice.

"What do you want me to do about it now? Call them up and say 'Oh, just kidding — we don't want you to come to our barbecue'?"

Mom cuts in. "It's just — I can't believe you invited them without asking me first."

When they come into the house, they speak in

hushed voices. I don't know why parents always do that. Do they really think we can't hear them?

"I'm sorry," says Dad. "But please know — this is important to me."

Mom sighs. "I know it is. But just think of it from their point of view. I grew up around people like them. I know what they're like. And from what you said the other night, Mr. — what's his name again?"

"Thomas. Bill Thomas."

"Right," she says. "Well, from what you said, he wasn't too friendly to you and Chris —"

One of my sisters lets out a screech. A fairy has just ripped someone's ear off. Abandoning their conversation — at least for now — my parents join us in the living room.

Dad points at the television. "Chris — why are you letting your sisters watch this?"

I hold up my hands. "It's about fairies."

He grabs the remote control and switches the screen off. "That movie was for us. The princess one was for your sisters."

How was I supposed to know?

The girls start begging him to let them see the rest of the film.

"No, no, no," says Dad. "And anyway, the Thomas family will be here soon. We are going to have a barbecue."

"Yay!" my sisters shout together.

Breaking Bread

"Chris, help your father get the groceries in," Mom says abruptly.

As I walk out to the car, my mind is swimming with questions. So — Dad invited Jason and his family over for a barbecue. Why is Mom so against the idea? And what did she mean by "people like them"? Is my own mother a racist, like Derek's father?

Of course not. My mom is a lawyer. She works for all different kinds of people. And — she married Dad. He isn't a white guy. He even comes from another country.

What's going on?

Dad seems to have purchased half the store again. Or half the barbecue aisle, anyway. It takes me three trips to bring everything into the house. Last is a huge, dusty bag of charcoal briquettes.

"Put those out by the barbecue," Dad tells me. "I'm going to make my famous kebabs."

That sounds great to me. But what about Jason and his family? They might not know what kebabs are. They might even be vegetarians.

After carrying everything through the house, I stay out in the backyard. I do sit-ups, push-ups, and some stretches. The city finals aren't until next week, but I need to be in tip-top shape.

Dad gets to work on the barbecue: heating the coals, slicing the meat and vegetables, sticking everything on skewers. He is just putting the kebabs on the grill when the doorbell rings.

There is the sound of voices inside the house. Then Mom comes through the back door, followed by Jason and his dad. A woman with shoulder-length black hair comes out after them with a baby fast asleep in her arms. Last is Jason's sister, Anna. She looks around shyly, but Lucy and Sarah are soon tugging at her hands, eager to show her around the backyard.

Jason's dad steps forward, holding out a paper bag. Dad reaches out and takes it. Looking inside, he chuckles. "Thank you. What a nice bottle of whiskey."

It is a warm autumn evening, so we sit outside. Mom puts three platefuls of flatbread on the picnic table with some salad and a big bowl of yogurt. Dad goes into full chef mode at the grill. The meat sizzles as he rotates his kebabs theatrically.

Pretty soon, everyone is digging in. The kebabs seem like a big hit, though I do catch Jason raising an eyebrow when he gets to the yogurt.

"It's a Persian thing," I tell him. "Yogurt goes with everything."

"Persian?" says Jason's mom to my dad. "You're from Iran?"

"Yes," Dad replies, looking down at his plate. "But I left a very long time ago."

"Well, the recipe might come from Iran," says Jason's dad, patting his stomach. "But this food is out of this world."

Jason dips a piece of lamb into some yogurt and takes a bite.

"Wow," he exclaims. "You were right, Chris. It really does go with everything."

When they are done eating, Lucy and Sarah make Anna join them in a game of hide-and-seek. She plays along good-naturedly, chasing them around the shrubs and the garden shed.

The dads take a walk to the edge of the yard. Jason and I are both still sitting at the picnic table, stuffing our faces, so we can't hear what they are talking about. My dad seems to be suggesting something. Jason's dad shakes his head at first. But then eventually, he begins to nod.

The moms sit together, watching the girls as they shriek and giggle. Jason's mom touches the back of my mom's hand. She points to the baby, who is reaching toward the sky with his little hands.

For the first time this evening, Mom's face softens into a warm smile.

12 THE END OF THE WORLD

I start my Sunday with an early run. It is a clear sunny morning, though a thin fog hangs above the trees. This reminds me of the smoke from the forest fires. It's hard to believe that was only a couple of weeks ago. It seems like another lifetime.

When I get back to the house, Dad is hauling stuff out of the garage.

"Chris," he says, squinting into the bright sunlight. "I'm glad you're back. There's something I need to talk to you about."

"What's that?"

He looks at me for a moment. "I forgot to tell you — Bill and I were talking last night. He and Jason are driving up-island today, back to — where they're from. Bill wants to do some work on their house."

I frown. "Didn't it burn down?"

Dad shakes his head. "Not entirely. Anyway, when I heard about it, I asked Bill if he needed some help.

He wasn't sure at first. But when I — explained my reasons, he said yes."

Dad continues. "We have to bring tents and sleeping bags. If you come, you'll miss two days of school. It's your choice. You don't have to come, Chris. But I really hope you will."

The first thing in my mind is the race. What about training? It would be two, maybe three, days without running. But on the other hand, Jason is my friend. He lost his home. That should be matter more to me, right?

"All right," I say. "I'll come."

Dad nods at me. "Fantastic. You've made the right decision."

Really, how could I give him any other answer?

"We leave in one hour," he tells me. "Get packing."

★★★

Through the pick-up truck's window, I see a long narrow beach that stretches all the way to the edge of the water. Beyond, the blue waves roll and shimmer under the midday sun.

A yawn escapes my throat. "Hey, Dad — where are we?"

He glances back over his shoulder. "I believe we are somewhere on the east coast of Vancouver Island."

Jason's dad chuckles. With one hand on the steering wheel, he points backward with his thumb. "We just passed through Ladysmith. Not even at Nanaimo yet. Still got a long way to go."

Jason is slumped next to me, hoodie pulled up over his head. From somewhere underneath there comes a long throaty snore. He looks more like a pile of clothes than an actual person.

The truck makes a big left turn away from the ocean. Soon, outside my window, there is nothing but trees. Trees, trees, and more trees. We drive on, a pair of teenage zombies conked out in the back seat and a pair of dads up front, drinking too much coffee. Mr. Thomas and my father launch back into one of their endless dad conversations. It travels from taxes to beards to hockey before I decide to listen to the hum of the engine and look out the window instead.

The trees here are incredible. They make ones in the Victoria look like tiny *bonsai* trees. I like heading deep into a forest. For one thing, the forest is usually where I win my races. Something about weaving back and forth between trees on a narrow winding path really gets my legs moving.

There is something else that gets them moving too. Horses, feathers, tomahawks, war paint —

I try to push those thoughts out of my mind. What is wrong with me? I am on my way to a First Nations reserve and *this* is what I am thinking about?

The truck slows down as we turn off the highway.

"Pit stop!" calls out Jason's dad from the front seat.

There is a monstrous growl next to me. The hoodie unzips. Out pops Jason, hair tangled and eyes bleary. "Are — are we there yet?"

I shake my head. "Just a pit stop."

"Good," he says. "Let's go get something to eat. I'm starving."

Before my dad can get his wallet out, Jason's dad hands us each ten bucks.

We have stopped at a gas station on the outskirts of a small town. I am just getting ready for a lunch of chocolate bars and potato chips when Jason points behind me.

"Look," he says. "A pancake restaurant!"

The place is so cheap that we can each afford two stacks of pancakes. They are light brown, doughy, and covered in sticky syrup. We scarf them down so fast that when we stand up to leave, the waitress gives us a funny look.

"You two aren't escaped criminals, are you?"

"Excuse me?" says Jason.

"Just the way you gobbled those pancakes. Cops on your tail?"

We barely make it out the front door before we burst out laughing.

"Dude," I say to Jason, "I think that waitress was hitting on you."

He wrinkles his nose. "Gross, man. She was older than my mom."

A horn beeps. Jason's dad has his hand out the truck's window, his finger tapping his watch.

"Race you," says Jason. He takes off running. I make sure to catch up, and then stay with him stride for stride.

Back in the truck, we drive on a smaller highway until we reach a junction. Here, the truck turns onto a bumpy road that heads inland toward the mountains.

Up front, the dads put some music on. But not good music. Their music. Music from before the dawn of time.

Jason nods in my direction. "Guess the city finals are this Friday, eh?"

"Uh — yeah," I say.

"You must be worried about missing training."

"Nah — not really," I say. I probably don't sound very convincing. "Though maybe I should be, after you beat me last race."

Jason shrugs. "Ah, come on — I got lucky. You were way ahead but then you stumbled."

When we left home, I was worried about missing training. But as soon as we got out of the city, my thoughts turned toward where we are going. What is a town like, after a disaster like this? Just a normal place, with damage here and there? Or is it like some post-apocalyptic movie, with basically no life left?

The End of the World

The thought is terrifying, but kind of exciting too.

The bumpy paved road we are on turns into an even bumpier dirt road. It is flanked by towering cedar trees, their trunks covered in thick green moss. Gigantic ferns sway in the breeze. I press my nose against the window. I have been in a forest before, but this is insane. Driving into these woods is almost like time travel. It looks like Jurassic Park.

We drive and drive. I don't know how we can go any further on this island without splashing into some water. At last, we come around a corner and there it is, the Pacific Ocean, big, blue and beautiful. It is different somehow from the ocean around Victoria. The waves here are massive. They heave upward before crashing down, pounding the shore like a mighty fist.

Beyond those waves, there is nothing, all the way to Japan.

"Welcome to the end of the world," says Jason.

13 THE PLACE BY THE SEA

"I'll be honest with you. I have heard many bad things about First Nations reserves," says my dad. "But this place — there are no words to describe how beautiful it is."

"Ah — you know how things work." Jason's dad shrugs. "On TV and the Internet, they only show the bad stuff. Don't get me wrong — there are real problems here. But this is a beautiful place. A good place."

"I feel the same way about Iran," says Dad. "There are many problems there too. But it is a wonderful country in so many ways. It is very different from what people in Canada and America think it is."

I have never heard Dad speak fondly of his country before, except for when he is talking about the food.

Suddenly, the trees around us change. No — they completely transform. Green leaves and needles disappear. Branches become blackened sticks. The bark on the trunks is cracked and grey. The ground itself seems like nothing but sick grey ash.

"*Khodaye man,*" says my father.

Oh my God is how you translate these words into English. But what my father really means is *I can't believe what I am seeing with my own two eyes.*

The first few buildings we pass seem to have escaped the flames. But then we see one house with its roof collapsed, followed by two houses with missing walls. And then we pass some places that are nothing but mounds of charred wood and blackened concrete.

I have to remember to breathe. It feels like all the air has been knocked out of me.

Jason stares out his window. His face is turned away. I can't imagine what is going through his mind.

The truck lurches to a stop.

"This is home," says Jason's dad.

There is a row of houses standing on the other side of the street. They look empty but normal, as if their owners are just away on vacation.

"I don't get it," mutters Jason. "How did the fire completely miss that side of the street?"

Turning around, I see Jason's dad walking toward a single-storey house. Or actually, half a single-storey house. I have never seen anything like it. It looks like a fiery axe came down from the sky and chopped it through the middle.

★★★

There is plenty of work to be done. For two and a half days, Jason and I use crowbars to rip down what is left of the garage. The place is badly damaged. Most of it ends up in a big pile of garbage out by the road. Once a day, a man in a big truck drives up and carts everything away.

On Tuesday, our last day, I see Jason bend forward to check out something on the ground. Since we got here, he has rarely stopped looking down. He walks around hunched over, as if the weight of what happened is too much to bear.

This time, he picks up something small and round. He holds it out for me to look at. It is a scuffed up orange ball, the kind used for street hockey.

"My buddies used to come over to the garage," says Jason, cradling the small orange sphere in his hands. "We would shoot these around for hours. Dad even put up a hockey net. Look, it's still here —"

He points at a piece of charred and twisted metal.

We keep working all afternoon, without a break. Eventually, Jason's dad comes over and makes us stop.

"Quitting time," he says. "Chris's dad is making dinner. Why don't you two go for a walk or something?"

Jason's body jerks upward. He looks at me intently. "A walk? Chris — let's go for a *run!*"

"Uh — okay," I say, surprised at the suggestion.

After changing into shorts and T-shirts in our

tents, we start off down the road. My feet feel like concrete blocks. My arms struggle to find their usual rhythm. Maybe it is all the heavy lifting I've been doing for the past three days. Or maybe it is everything that I have seen.

It doesn't take us long to reach the end of the street, which is really the end of the town. From there, a narrow dirt path winds its way into the forest. The only sounds in my ears are our shoes hitting the dirt and the thumping of my own heart. Gradually they are joined by another sound: a low rumble, like thunder. My arms and legs lose their stiffness. We are really running now, flying through the forest.

The trees here seem to have escaped the fire. A few are black around their trunks — from the smoke, I guess — but above us is a roof of brown and green.

Jason slows down as we come around a massive boulder. The wind picks up, blowing hard against us, so hard that at first I turn away. When I look up, I see that we are standing on a rocky beach. The low rumble has become a crashing boom, as massive waves beat down on jagged rocks.

Chest heaving, Jason points at something behind me. At first all I see are a group of trees without branches. But then I realize that they are not trees at all.

"Totem poles!" I blurt out. "Real totem poles!"

I think of the Royal BC Museum in Victoria. That place is stuffed with totem poles. I have seen them many times. And yet here, with the wind and waves, these ones seem different. It feels like these totem poles have always been here. This is the place where they belong.

We walk over to take a closer look. These are old. Some are barely standing. One has a crack running down it from top to bottom, right through the eyes of what might be a bear. Or it could be a whale or even a human being, for all I can tell.

"Don't they ever repair these?" I ask.

Jason shakes his head. "Nah — we let them fall down, then we build new ones. That's the traditional way, I think."

"You think?"

He laughs. "I've always been too busy dreaming of playing in the NHL to care what some elder or teacher was saying about history or tradition. I do know the Nuu-chah-nulth word for totem pole, though."

He says the word twice. I try to repeat it, but end up choking on my tongue.

"Sorry."

Jason laughs. "Don't stress. I've heard how Ms. Taylor butchers your last name. Actually it's one of the only Nuu-chah-nulth words I know. Sure wish I knew more."

"I know what you mean. My dad's language is Farsi. I kind of understand it, but I can't speak it very well."

I look up at the totem poles once more.

"The fire came in the middle of the night," says Jason. "My dad rushed into my room and pulled me out of bed. I helped my mom and my sister. Dad carried the baby. We sprinted down that path all the way to this beach. When we looked back, all we could see were the flames behind us."

I think of all my races, all those imagined dangers behind me. They seem so silly, now that I have met someone who actually had to run for his life.

14 THE BIG RACE

When I go back to school on Wednesday, the guys bombard me with questions.

"Did you see that school that burned down?" Derek asks, eyes blazing.

"Yeah," I tell him. "I saw it."

He nods, looking satisfied.

"Did you see any torched cars?" asks someone else.

There is no way to tell the guys, not even Yongwon or Sparky, about the totem poles or the amazing *Jurassic Park* forest. Or even the hockey ball that Jason found in the ruins of his garage. All they want to hear is confirmation of the destruction that they have already seen on TV and the Internet.

For the next few days, Victoria feels strange to me. Every morning, on my way to school, I pause to look around. Until recently, I always felt far away from bad news. Wars, earthquakes, tsunamis — that kind of stuff. Bad news was something that happened somewhere else, to someone else.

The Big Race

But now I know that disaster can strike anywhere. What if half the houses on my block burned to the ground? What would that do to me and my family?

At school, I am barely aware of which class I am in. Math, French, Social Studies — they all seem kind of pointless, detached from the real world. All I can think about is Jason's hometown, and everything I saw in those three days.

"What's up, Chris?" asks Yongwon on Friday afternoon. I am doodling shapes around a math equation that I should be solving.

He tries again when I don't reply. "I guess you're focusing on the big race after school today, huh?"

It isn't like I have forgotten the city finals. Winning them has been my dream since I was eight years old. But the race is kind of sneaking up on me. I guess that is what happens when you have other things on your mind.

"Yeah," I say to Yongwon. "Something like that."

"Just don't lose to Jason again," he says. "He's quick for a big guy."

I'm not sure how I feel about racing against Jason anymore. My whole life, all I have wanted is to finish in first place, out in front of everybody else. Right now, that doesn't seem quite so important.

I don't see Jason that day until after school, out on the soccer field. We have both changed into our running uniforms, in the school colours of red and black. He is wearing the same old worn-out sneakers that are always on his feet. In his right hand, he holds something round and orange.

"The street hockey ball," I say.

He spins it around in his fingers. "Yeah — I thought it might bring me some luck. Sort of like whatever you are running away from when you race."

Guilt rushes into me. I can feel it rising up from my stomach to my throat.

"Hey — listen," I say to him, forcing out the words. "This is going to sound terrible. But — well, you know the first day I met you? I had just finished a run. You said it looked like I had been running from the cops or something."

Jason grins. "Yeah, man. You couldn't stop looking over your shoulder."

I know that he might not be smiling for very long. After he hears what I have to say, there is a good chance he will never want to speak to me again. But I have to tell him.

"When I run," I begin, "I imagine being chased — by someone or something. Like, for motivation."

He looks at me. "Yeah? So what? Nothing wrong with that. Whatever makes you run faster."

I shake my head. "Yeah, but after I heard you guys would be coming to our school, I started imagining — your people. Native people. I mean — First Nations people. But, they weren't real people. They were these bloodthirsty savages on horses waving tomahawks. You know, like in old black-and-white cowboy movies. Look — I know it's terrible. I'm not proud of it."

Jason stares at me. I wonder if he is deciding whether to punch me. After all those years playing hockey, one punch would mean the end of my face.

Instead, Jason reaches out and shoves me backward. "You were worried about telling me *that*? Come on, man — that's weak. It's just your dumb imagination. I know you don't think my family and I are bloodthirsty savages." He stops and thinks. "I would like to have my own tomahawk, though. Those things look pretty awesome in the movies. But there is no way my mom would let me have something so dangerous!"

This guy should be swearing at me. Or least calling me names. But he just stands there, looking amused. Why do I feel almost disappointed?

"Remember my first day here?" Jason asks. "When Yongwon asked what kind of music my band plays? You see — that kind of stuff doesn't bother me. Yongwon wasn't trying to be mean. He just didn't know. It wasn't hurting anyone. It was actually pretty funny."

His eyes narrow as he goes on. "Chris, Yongwon is not the kind of person who worries me. And neither are you. Look — I know exactly who egged my house and scared my family that night. That's the kind of person we have to worry about."

Should I ask him who egged his house?

I don't get the chance to decide because at that moment Greg Sparks appears next to us,

"Ready, guys?" he gulps. His hands are shaking. "One, two, three finish today, right?"

"You got it," says Jason. "One, two, three — Sparky, Chris, and me."

"Not in *that* order," says Sparky, turning red.

We follow the crowd of students, parents, and teachers across the field to the edge of the Jungle. Around the starting line, runners are stretching their muscles, retying their laces, warming up their legs.

I see Coach Clark over by the spectators. Two women and one man are standing right in front of her, gesturing in our direction as she tries to explain something to them.

"What's that all about?" asks Sparky.

At last, Coach Clark breaks away from them, shaking her head. As she walks toward the three of us, she looks pale and shaken.

"Honestly," she hisses. "People here make me sick sometimes."

"What happened?" asks Jason.

She looks at him. "They're parents of kids at our school. The same parents who were happy to send charity stuff to your reserve. Now, they are upset because you are running in the race and their kids are not."

The Big Race

Jason takes a step back. "Hey — I don't want to step on anyone's toes. Maybe it's better if I don't run."

"No way," says Coach Clark. "You earned your place in this race. I'm not letting a small group of busybodies come in and mess things up."

Over her shoulder, I see Ms. Taylor walking this way. She moves quickly across the rough ground for someone wearing such high heels.

This does not look good.

"Melissa," she says to Coach Clark. "Can I have a word, please? It's urgent."

Before Coach Clark can say a word, I step out in front of her. "If Jason doesn't run, Sparky and I don't run either."

A man with a megaphone cuts in. "All runners — all runners report to the starting line."

For a moment that lasts forever, Ms. Taylor stares at me. It's as if she doesn't believe that I dared to speak up. But then something changes in her face. She waves a hand in front of us.

"You're right. Of course you're right. Go run your race, you three."

She turns to Coach Clark. "Forget about it. I'll deal with the parents."

"Great," says Sparky. "Now we only have to worry about the other guys in the race."

We step up to the starting line. It is a big crowd today. Yongwon is there with the whole basketball team. Angeli and Helen, wearing the school colours, are cheering and clapping their hands. Mom is down at the far end, holding hands with Sarah and Lucy. And — could that really be him? But he never comes to my races.

Next to my sisters is my dad.

I take my place in the group of runners. How many are there — thirty-five, forty? This is a big race.

"Runners, ready!"

The gravel crunches under my shoes.

"On your marks. Set. Go!"

15 BOXED IN

I launch myself forward, and smack into an elbow. It knocks me sideways. I stagger onward, eyes bleary. What a terrible start.

Not terrible, just unlucky. Never mind. Keep going.

I focus on my feet, on my arm movements, on keeping up with the group. My vision clears as we reach the first bend in the trail.

That is when I realize that something strange is going on. The guys on all sides of me are wearing the same blue uniforms. Those uniforms are from St. Mary's Academy, a private boys' school just outside Oak Bay.

I take a few quick strides, trying to break free. The runners around me close in. One on my right bumps me with his shoulder. I swear under my breath, but there is not much I can do. There are five or six of them. I am surrounded. They have me boxed in.

That elbow at the starting line was no accident.

When we get into the Jungle, things gets nastier.

There are course marshals every few hundred metres to make sure no one gets lost or takes a shortcut. But the St. Mary's boys bide their time, waiting until the marshals are out of sight. I take two more elbows and three shoulder-barges by the time we are out of the trees. I feel like a punching bag.

One thing is now obvious. These guys planned this in advance. But why? Maybe they looked at my running times in the qualifiers and decided I was the biggest threat. But if they did that, wouldn't Jason be the one they would want to box in? He was the one who finished first.

We pass the start line again and begin lap two. I see Sarah pressing buttons on Mom's phone. Lucy and Mom are cheering and jumping up and down. Dad is just sitting there, hands in his lap. He raises a hand to wave at me as I run past.

In front of the crowd, the guys in blue ease up a little bit. Ahead of us, I see Sparky and the Man in Black running neck and neck. Rocket-Shoes is up there too. Beside him is a blond guy in a blue St. Mary's uniform. Suddenly, everything makes sense.

The trail dips downward and we head back into the Jungle. Right away, an elbow digs me in the ribs. Oof — that one hurt. I'm not sure how much more of this I can take.

Come on, I tell myself. *You've made it this far, all the way to the city finals. Don't you dare give up now.*

Boxed In

Bump. Grunt. Thump. Elbow.

One guy actually tries to trip me, but I manage to sidestep. He stumbles and falls. But it is a small victory. There are just too many of them, and they aren't letting up.

I am been so busy dealing with my police escort — the blue uniforms around me — that I almost forget about Jason. He doesn't seem to be up with Sparky and Rocket-Shoes and the other leaders. Maybe he's way out front. Or maybe something happened to him, a fall or a sprained ankle. I sure hope not.

"Go, Chris!" shouts Dad as I finish my second lap. He is totally into the race now. He is up on his feet, pumping his fists in the air. Under his T-shirt, his belly shakes up and down. It is as if his whole body wants me to win this race.

Come on, Chris. There has got to be a way out of this.

Back we go into the Jungle, one last time. Shoulder to shoulder, elbow to ribs, and finally, a slap to the face. If there is a way out, I sure can't see it.

One of them growls at me. "Why don't you just quit? We've got you totally boxed in."

In a race, everything flows in one direction. One-way traffic. And so it is a shock when we turn a corner and something — someone — is barrelling straight toward us.

Jason.

No one has time to react. The guy next to me is

knocked flying into a bush. Two others slip and fall over. A gap opens up in front of me, between two runners.

"Go!" shouts Jason. "Run for your life!"

The blue uniforms try to move together and close me in. Powering forward, I push my way between them and take off.

Footsteps pound the path behind me. My pursuers have not given up. But for once in my life, I don't worry about that. I think about the curves through the rest of trees, then the long straightaway, and the climb to the finish line — where my friends and my coach and my family will be cheering me all the way.

But first, I have some runners to chase down.

Feet kicking up dirt behind me, I shift into top gear. The Man in Black appears in front of me. He is limping as he runs. It looks like he has a cramp.

"Keep going, man," I say. I give him a pat on the back.

He calls something out after me, but I can't make it out. He could be thanking me. He could be telling me to go jump in a lake.

I catch up to Sparky at the beginning of the long straight stretch. He is red-faced, nose snorting air like the intake of a sputtering engine. But Rocket-Shoes is just a few strides ahead.

"Come on, Sparky," I say. "Me, Jason and you —1-2-3!"

A smile, or a grimace, flickers over his lips. "Not — in that — order."

No, I think to myself. But Jason has done something unbelievable. He has given us both a chance. We can't let him down now.

I surge ahead, pulling Sparky along with me. Rocket-Shoes tries for a final burst, but his burners are all burned out. He swears at us as we cut around him.

"Eat my dust, dude!" shouts Sparky, then he mumbles to me, "I've been eating his dust all race."

We are almost at the bottom of the hill. Up ahead is the blond guy in the blue uniform. He is moving slower now, but he is already close to the top.

"Come on — Sparks," I say. "Let's run that jerk into the ground."

He stares ahead with wide exhausted eyes. "Chris — thanks for everything, man. But you go. I'll see you — at the finish line."

When my feet hit the hill, I try to picture something shadowy behind me, chasing me down. My mind flicks through pirates, ghosts, and savages. I even imagine a forest fire. But then I see my sisters — Sarah too — clapping and my mom on her feet. I see my dad cheering. I hear Yongwon and Helen and Angeli screaming my name.

And that, it turns out, is all I need. Together, their voices pull me up the hill, past the blond kid, and over the finish line.

First place.

Collapsing onto the dirt, I turn just in time to see Sparky crossing the line. And behind him, neck and neck with the blond kid, is one more red and black uniform.

"Go, Jason!" shouts Sparky.

All I can do is hold my breath.

Jason cranes his neck as he crosses the finish line. The judges point to him. Third place.

Our friends and families charge toward us. Three teammates at the finish line, 1-2-3. Never mind the order.

In the grass at the side of the track rests an orange hockey ball, silent but proud.

16 GOING BACK

It's been a week since the city finals. I am half-asleep on the living room couch when the front door flies open and *something* bursts into our house.

Coughing and sputtering, the thing tugs off an ancient red T-shirt. It has a big round belly and its chest is heaving like a huge accordion. Its whole body is covered in thick black hair. Is it human? Is it beast? Or is it a bad dream? It could be a Sasquatch. But surely even a Sasquatch wouldn't be caught dead in neon orange shorts and matching running shoes.

I sit up sharply. "Dad? What on earth are you doing?"

He uses the ancient T-shirt to wipe away some of the sweat. His face is almost as red as his shirt. I have never seen anyone so sweaty before.

"Did you go swimming in the ocean or something?"

He is still too out of breath to respond. I run to the bathroom to grab him a towel.

"Thanks," he wheezes back at me. "Wow — I am out of shape."

Off he goes to take a shower. I am left standing in the living room, shaking my head. What have I just witnessed?

"Lunch time, everyone," Mom calls from the kitchen.

I sit at the table next to my sisters. Lunch is tomato soup and tuna sandwiches. Mom's cooking isn't as fancy as Dad's. But the sandwiches taste okay, and the soup is really good.

"What is Dad up to?" I ask, setting down my glass of water.

She rolls her eyes. "I think he will want to tell you himself."

Dad joins us moments later. His hair is wet from the shower. His face is a little less red.

"Chris was just asking what you're up to," says Mom. She hands him a sandwich and a bowl of soup.

Dad smiles, a mischievous glint in his eyes. "Your race last week inspired me. I have decided that I will run a half-marathon next year. Training began today."

Sarah looks at Dad like he has just announced he plans to fly to Jupiter. "But you're fat, Daddy. Fat people can't run marathons. Not even half-marathons."

"Not even quarter-marathons," adds Lucy.

"Well," replies Dad. "If I keep training, maybe I won't be fat for long. Daddy wasn't always fat, you know —"

Going Back

Lucy and Sarah stare at him as if he has just told them that the moon no longer exists.

The doorbell rings. The girls race off together to answer the door. When they return, Jason is with them.

Something looks different about him today. Normally he stands upright, facing the world like a soldier. Today, shoulders slumped, his whole body droops. With a long, deep breath, he wipes his eyes on his sleeve.

"Girls," says Mom. "Go outside and play."

They leave, but Jason doesn't say anything. He sits down at the table across from Dad and me. Mom brings him a glass of water.

"I just found out today," he finally says. "We're going back."

Mom puts a hand on his shoulder. "Oh — really? But that's a good thing, right?"

He nods, but there are tears in his eyes. "Yeah — of course it is. My parents don't like it here in Victoria. They aren't city people. And — I do miss my buddies back home."

He gulps down some water. "This — this whole thing has been really hard, you know? I want to go back. But at the same time, I wish I could stay. It's complicated."

Mom looks as if she is about to say something again, but Dad speaks first.

"I think I understand," he says quietly. "I know what it is like to leave your home and wonder if you can ever go back. And, even if you do, you wonder if home can ever be the same as it was before."

Mom stands up. She takes a step toward Dad.

He holds up his hand. "It's okay. I want to talk about it."

Jason's eyes are dry now. Like me, he is wondering what is going on.

Dad sets his coffee cup down on the table. "I have never told you, Chris, why I left Iran. I always said that I came here as an exchange student, met your mom, and decided to stay."

He pauses before he continues. "The truth is — I never wanted to leave Iran. The heat of the desert, the saltiness of the Caspian Sea, the mountains behind the city of Tehran — I loved living in Iran. My friends and I played soccer three or four times a week. One of them had a father who owned a restaurant with the sweetest tea in the city. We used to go there after games. He would give us glass after glass of tea and then feed us until we couldn't stand up."

He takes a deep breath. "But there were big changes in the country. Political changes. I didn't care much at first. I was just a young guy. I had been working for the university newspaper, but nothing political — just articles on sports, mostly. So I kept playing soccer and drinking tea and eating with my friends. But then one day, these men came to my house. They warned my father, 'Get your son out of the country.' I never found out exactly why. My father acted at once. His brother was living here, in Victoria. Two days later, I was on a plane. And I have never been back."

The kitchen is silent. Because what can you say, after hearing something like that?

A shadow falls over Dad's face. "When I arrived in Canada, I could barely speak English. The food was strange. I didn't know anyone — only my uncle. And not everyone was nice to me. There were some real jerks. One man even told me to go back to Africa."

That makes all of us laugh.

"I bet that idiot failed geography class," says Jason.

Dad nods. "Other people helped me, though. Not just with clothes or food or basic things like that. They helped me learn the language. They introduced me to fast food. They became my friends. I even found a place to play soccer again. And Victoria became my home."

Mom lifts her head and speaks. "I worried about Al being so eager to help your family, Jason. I knew he meant well, but I was worried about how your mom and dad would feel. Nobody likes to be given things that other people don't need. It's not a good feeling. Especially for people from your — community."

Suddenly things make more sense to me. My mom is no racist. She was concerned about Dad. She was worried that he would be hurt by the reaction of Jason's family.

But she was wrong. Yes, Dad did try to give them things — pasta sauce and clothing and, unfortunately, whiskey. But in the end, he gave them far, far more. And now, I understand why.

Dad stands up. "I'm sorry. You came over here with important news. I have taken up all your time with my old stories."

Jason shakes his head. "No way, Mr. Khalili. Thank you for telling me that story. If it's okay with you, I'll share it with my dad later."

"Of course," says Dad, with a warm smile. "And thank you for pronouncing our family name correctly. That doesn't happen very often."

After Mom and Dad leave the kitchen, Jason turns toward me.

"There is something else I have to tell you," he says. "It's about the eggs and the insults. It was Derek, you know. Derek and his brothers."

Part of me knew it was Derek all along. Hearing it confirmed sets my blood boiling. "I'm going to kick the crap out of that guy —"

Jason shakes his head. "Nah. I want you to forget about that. Guys like Derek and his brothers — they're like those guys who told your Iranian dad to go back to Africa. I feel sorry for them, really. That kind of guys are the same, wherever you go. And in the end, they miss out on a lot."

I think I understand. Most of my friends are

guys who I've grown up with, right here in this neighbourhood. Guys pretty much like me. Over the past few weeks, I got to know someone who I never would have met in my normal life. Jason only comes from the other side of Vancouver Island, but it's pretty much another world. And now, we are friends. I am glad I didn't miss out on that.

EPILOGUE

The path is never straight, never flat — never easy. The soft black dirt crumbles under the soles of my shoes. Thick roots stretch out like sneaky legs, trying to catch my toes. Wet green leaves reach out to slap me in the face.

But I don't stop. Provincial championships are coming up. This is no time to slack off.

Jason sent a message to my phone the other day:

See you at provincials. Don't expect any charity from me!

It sure will be good to see him. But he'd better be ready to run the race of his life.

I continue through the forest until a gap in the trees opens up. I hear the pounding of the surf. I feel the wind on my skin. I see the ancient totem poles, rising from the stony ground.

There is no point looking back. Eyes forward, I keep going. Running into tomorrow. Running for my life.

ACKNOWLEDGEMENTS

This book could never have been completed without the support and encouragement of my family, friends, and colleagues. Kat Mototsune, my editor at Lorimer, helped me immeasurably through the many significant changes that the book went through. Monica Pacheco, my agent at Anne McDermid and Associates, helped with the business side of things so that I could remain focused on my writing. I would like to thank my colleagues and students at Yokohama International School, in particular Melissa Hamada for her expert advice on the nuances of trail running. The irrepressible James Midgley made clear to me that jogging and running are most definitely *not* the same, and his lifelong dedication to the latter inspired me to get writing, and running too! My students Lars and Morgan also sparked my interest in running through their own obsessions with cross-country running and through an excellent book recommendation: *Born to Run* by Christopher McDougall. To Marjan and Ali, my Farsi language consultants, *mersi*. And to my wife, Misako, and my little boy, Tony — thank you most of all for your love, your laughter, and your patience.